Bergerac loosed off a round from his Smith and Wesson, but the two fleeing figures ahead continued running and disappeared into the house.

He jumped down from the wall and, covered by the marksmen, tugged open the heavy gates. The harsh clangour of the alarm erupted from the house. Crozier, Goddard and the other two policemen edged through the gate.

'We can't rush the house,' Bergerac told Crozier. 'Not with Bailey and the housekeeper in there.'

Crozier nodded. 'Right. Everyone fan out and take cover.'

Behind them they could hear the sirens of police reinforcements coming up the cliff road. From the house came the tinkle of glass from upstairs windows . . .

By the same author

Eh Brian, It's a Whopper

IMPRIMÉ EN FRANCE

ANDREW SAVILLE

Bergerac

Crimes of the Season

*Based on the television series
created by
Robert Banks Stewart*

PANTHER
Granada Publishing

Panther Books
Granada Publishing Ltd
8 Grafton Street, London W1X 3LA

Published by Panther Books 1985

This novelization based on the television scripts
What Dreams by Brian Finch, *Return of the Ice-Maiden*
by Rod Beacham and *The Last Interview* by
Robert Banks Stewart

ISBN 0-586-06815-5

Made and printed for
William Collins Sons & Co. Ltd, Glasgow

Set in Times

Chapter 1

It was a room with a view.

Through the plate-glass picture window you could stare down on a forest of concrete and brick. Never-ending streams of brightly coloured traffic threaded their way between the buildings. Between some of the buildings you could see the glint of water, where the Hudson ran into the grey waters of the Atlantic. Down below, eight million New Yorkers were going about their business.

It was a view which had cost a great deal of money.

But none of the three people in the office was looking at it. All of them were staring at the tape recorder on the corner of the desk. An air-conditioner hummed in the background. Sound-proofing filtered out the street sounds of Manhattan Island. The woman and the two men were leaning a fraction forward in their seats, concentrating on the gruff voice which was coming through the tape recorder's loudspeaker.

'They're still trying to find me, that's for goddam sure. They never give up, including them that went to gaol. How long since we met, Howard? Must be two, three years, huh?'

The voice had the rusty inflection of American-Italian. It was as blunt as a sawn-off shotgun, and sounded just as ugly.

There was a throaty sigh before the speaker continued. 'It's gone quick. I haven't seen your mug on the TV screen lately, but I guess you know they don't run programmes like yours on the local station here. Just news, and all the crappy old cop shows and even crappier movies.'

A brief pause followed, as if the man was trying to collect his thoughts. Arlene Roskin, the woman who sat behind the huge desk, glanced across at Joe Conte. He was a grey-haired man with an immaculate dark suit and the glossy patina of a successful professional. He held her gaze for an instant and gave a tiny nod.

'Listen, Howard.' The voice had now acquired an edge of urgency, almost panic. 'I'm sending this tape to you care of the network. Lemme give it to you straight: I'm dying. Yeah, right, dying with the big C. Jeez, I wish the Guy Upstairs would gimme a break. But yesterday I checked the X-rays myself. I'm out of luck. Maybe a couple of months at the most. Ironic, don't you think? My old friends would kill me on the spot if they knew where I was and who I was nowadays. Seems like I'm saving them the bother.'

Vince, the third occupant of the room, eased himself out of his leather-upholstered armchair and walked over to the desk. He was much younger than Conte, but already there was a hint of puffiness marring his lean, dark good looks. He picked up the photograph which lay beside the tape recorder and studied it intently.

It showed two men, sitting on either side of a table. They were in the open air. Beyond them was the blue of the sea. The sea could have been anywhere from the Pacific to the Mediterranean. Tony Abellini, the speaker on the tape, was sitting on the left, with a radio microphone pinned to his lapel. He was squat, balding and elderly – and as unmistakably Italian as a bottle of Chianti.

The man facing him was a complete contrast. Howard Bailey was in his early forties, but he had retained the youthful looks which had misled so many of the people he had interviewed. He was a quiet-spoken Englishman with a talent for making his interviewees say things they later regretted. Ten or twelve years ago he had tricked an

6

unintended admission out of a man in the White House; since then he had been an international celebrity.

Vince's eyes flicked from the photograph to the tape recorder. 'Anyhow,' Abellini was saying, 'that's why I want this favour – one last interview with the best guy in the business. I wanna put a few more nails in their coffin before they nail *me* down for good. Think of it: Howard Bailey cross-examines Tony Abellini again.' There was a chuckle which was submerged in a fit of coughing. 'The final curtain. You're the only one I'll talk to, Howard. The only guy in the world who knows where I am. Whaddya say? Some show, huh?'

Joe Conte leant forward and pushed the stop button. For a moment, the only sound in the office was the muted whirr of the air-conditioner. Arlene Roskin studied her perfectly manicured nails. She was an attractive woman in her early thirties; she dressed with a glossy femininity which only partially concealed the stainless steel beneath. A girl had to be tough to survive in New York's executive jungle.

She broke the silence with an appreciative but entirely ladylike whistle. 'Some show, all right.'

'Some curtain,' Conte said drily.

Arlene touched the gold table-lighter on her desk as if it were a talisman. 'But it'll have to be handled very carefully, Joe.'

Conte nodded. 'You can handle it.' For an instant his eyes locked on Arlene's.

Vince let the photograph flutter from his fingers on to the desk. 'Howard Bailey will take a lot of persuading,' he warned. 'He's turned down offers from every television network for over a year. He's quit.'

Conte ejected the cassette from the machine and held it up between his finger and thumb. 'This'll persuade him. Plus the biggest fee he's ever been offered.'

7

'He's a millionaire,' Arlene objected. 'Money won't necessarily help.'

Conte gave a cynical shrug: in his world, money always helped. 'Half the fee up-front, in cash? Even a millionaire would find that hard to resist.'

Vince tapped the photograph. 'I thought Bailey had gone to ground for his own reasons, like Abellini. You know where he is?'

Arlene nodded. 'Jersey.'

'New Jersey?' Vince sounded incredulous. '*That* close?'

'No of course not,' said Conte testily. 'It's the island in the English Channel which gave the state its name – '

The telephone rang, cutting him off in mid-sentence. Arlene pounced on it. She listened for a moment and then said, 'Right, put him through.' She covered the mouthpiece with her free hand and looked across the desk at the two men. 'It's him.' There was a flash of excitement in her eyes. 'My secretary finally managed to trace his number.'

The phone crackled in her ear. Arlene whipped her hand away from the mouthpiece. 'Hello? Howard?' Her voice suddenly had a warmth which verged on the seductive. 'That you?' Simultaneously she flicked the switch which coupled the telephone with the external speaker.

'Yes, Howard Bailey speaking.' There was a trace of irritation in the familiar British voice. 'Who *is* this?'

'Arlene – Arlene Roskin.'

'Who?' The irritation was no longer just a trace.

'Vice-President of Original Programming.' Arlene smiled into the phone. 'We met at the network when Morton Huberman did this job. You remember?'

'Of course I remember Morton.' Bailey paused. 'And what can I do for you, Miss Roskin?'

'Tony Abellini's been in touch. He sent us a tape. More specifically, he sent the tape to you. He wants to

8

do another interview. And you're the only guy he'll trust to do it.'

Arlene swiftly outlined the circumstances, using all her considerable powers of persuasion. When she finished, there was silence at the other end of the line. At least the guy hadn't put the phone down. 'Howard? You still there?'

'Look, you know perfectly well that I'm out of the game now,' Bailey snapped. 'Completely – no more assignments of any kind. If you don't know why, Morton Huberman does.'

'I talked with him.' Arlene sounded as if she was coaxing a fractious child. 'This is something *special*.'

'No it isn't.' Bailey's voice hardened. 'Get it into your head – I'm through. I'm sorry for Abellini – as much as anyone can feel sorry for an ex-Mafia gangster. But you'll have to forget me. Find yourself another interviewer.'

'But we need *you*. For a start, you're the only one who knows where he is, the only – '

'Certainly not.'

'Oh come on, Howard,' Arlene pleaded. 'Everyone here at the network wants you to do it. It'll make one helluva show – we can go worldwide by satellite on this one. And that means we pay you the highest figure you – '

'Save your breath and your phone bill,' Bailey interrupted. 'The answer is no. Goodbye.'

There was a click as he put the phone down. Arlene gently replaced the handset. She looked across the expanse of her desk at the two men. Her face was impassive. The only sound in the office was the whirr of the air-conditioner.

Sergeant Jim Bergerac glanced down at the temperature gauge in the dash of the Triumph Roadster. The car wasn't enjoying this stop-start, low-gear drive through

9

the crowded streets of St Helier, any more than he was. And it could be awkward if the Triumph chose this moment to overheat. Barney Crozier's opinions about Bergerac's unorthodox choice of transport were well-known; and a breakdown now would give the Inspector the ammunition he needed.

Bergerac changed down again and checked that his quarry was still moving in the same direction. At least Caulfield was easy to keep under surveillance: he was a tall, heavily-built man, large enough to stick out among the other pedestrians. He looked like a prosperous businessman on the fringe of middle age – which, Bergerac thought, was precisely what he was. The briefcase was still in his right hand.

Caulfield paused outside one of the entrances to the Victorian covered market, an impressive building of dressed granite, cast iron and glass which attracted tourists as well as the locals. Caulfield's head moved. He was probably trying to check if anyone in the street had stopped when he did. Bergerac drove on at exactly the same speed. Caulfield turned into the market.

Bergerac pulled up at the kerb on the opposite side of the road. He was just outside an estate agent's, he noticed with wry amusement: *how convenient*. He pulled the small walkie-talkie out of his pocket, and spoke quietly into it.

'Barry? He's just turned into the market.'

Detective Constable Goddard's reply came almost immediately. 'Yeah. I got him, Jim.'

Bergerac heaved a silent sigh of relief. It was always a risk, that moment when a suspect was out of sight of one pursuer and hadn't been picked up by the second. 'The stuff's in his briefcase. I saw him make the pick-up. I'll take this exit. Everyone else in position?'

'Yeah.' Goddard paused. 'But it could be a while

before he starts trading. He's gone into that café by the fountain. Looks like he's having a nosh.'

'Okay,' Jim said grimly. 'We'll wait.'

It was at times like this that Bergerac wished he still smoked. After you had picked your nose and drummed your fingers against the steering-wheel a few times, there wasn't a lot more you could do. Besides, the odds were that he wouldn't be needed: Wilson and the other men knew what they were doing.

The seconds lengthened into minutes. Bergerac looked away from the entrance to the market and stared at the properties in the estate agent's window. As he watched, a very pretty girl came round to the narrow space between the window and the boards on which the particulars of the houses were displayed.

Bergerac craned across to get a better view. Not exactly a girl – in her early thirties, maybe. But still very pretty. She was unpinning one of the colour photographs. Just before she left, the photograph in her hand, she glanced back, looking directly at Bergerac. He tried the effect of a small smile. It was hard to tell if there was any response.

He looked back to the entrance to the market. There was no sign of Caulfield and the radio was quiet. A grin flickered across his usually stern face, making him briefly seem much younger. He got out of the car and walked over to the window.

The display boards blocked his vision. He bent down so he could peer between the legs of the stands which supported them. The woman was sitting at a desk at the back of the showroom, scribbling away industriously. Bergerac rapped on the window.

The woman looked up with a start. He could read her hesitation on her face: was this a potential customer – or just some lunatic trying a novel way of picking her up? Bergerac added to her confusion, first by beckoning her

11

to come outside, and then by turning away to stare across at the entrance to the covered market.

'Our customers usually come inside.' Her voice was attractive as well. '*If* you're a customer.'

Bergerac allowed himself the luxury of a quick glance. She was framed in the doorway and looked even more attractive at this close range. Bergerac tore his eyes away. 'I can't come in,' Bergerac said abruptly. 'Not right now.'

'Why not?'

Bergerac jerked his thumb towards the market. 'I'm supposed to be watching that entrance. We're trying to trap a drug-pusher. There's a man on each exit.' He looked up again; he could tell she was curious now. 'I'm a copper.'

As he knew only too well, members of the public generally found it hard to find the appropriate response to that particular admission. He decided to soften the blow.

'As I happened to be lounging outside your window, I saw one of your properties which would be just right for me.' He pointed to one of the photographs. 'That one. The flat in Grouville.'

'Sorry. That was sold five minutes ago.' There was a hint of amusement in her voice.

Bergerac pulled a mock scowl. 'While I've been hanging around outside! That's life, isn't it?'

She gave a snort of laughter. 'Look, if you came in, you could still keep an eye on the market from our window. Then I could take your details, Mr . . ?'

'Bergerac. Sergeant Jim Bergerac.' He smiled up at her, liking the way she was insisting on going on with her job, just as he was with his. He quickly assessed the pros and cons of her suggestion and then nodded. 'After you.'

He followed her into the shop but chose a position near the door which gave him an unimpeded view of the market. In the rear of the showroom was an older man, presumably the manager, fiddling with the controls of a video. He was talking with an affluent-looking middle-aged couple, probably from the mainland, but glanced over towards the door as Bergerac came in. The man's expression as he turned back to the couple reflected his opinion of Bergerac's likely bank balance.

The woman settled herself at the desk nearest the door, pulled out a form and noted down Bergerac's name and address. The TV screen linked with the video came to life. Bergerac caught a glimpse of what looked like a Georgian manor house set in expensively landscaped grounds. The camera tracked inside the house. The agent's voice rose in his excitement.

'All the rooms in the house overlook either the pool or the charming courtyard and fountain. And here you can see that the main drawing-room connects with the pool-side pavilion . . .'

Bergerac looked down at the woman at the same moment as she looked up at him. Their shared opinion of the manager instantly made them conspirators. 'Bet you don't video my sort of place.'

The woman gave a demure smile. 'No. You get shown over personally. Let's see, where are you at the moment?'

'A cottage inland from Gorey in Queen's Valley,' Bergerac said absently, his eyes back on the road. 'Old vineyard building. It's under compulsory purchase order.'

'Where they're flooding for the new reservoir?'

Bergerac nodded. He noticed that a sign on the desk displayed the woman's name: Susan Young.

'The flat in the window was thirty-eight thousand,' she continued. 'What's your ceiling?'

'Thirty.' Bergerac saw her expression and added: 'I'd have tried to beat you down, wouldn't I?' The radio bleeped in his pocket. 'Hang on a minute.'

He pulled out the radio, switching it to receive. Susan looked politely away. Goddard's voice crackled softly:

13

'Jim, I think he may be about to do a little business at last
. . . Damn! The other bloke's sussed me. Jim, Caulfield's
beelining for your exit.'

Bergerac had his hand on the door handle before the
radio went silent. 'Sorry,' he flung back over his shoulder.
'Emergency.'

Susan called after him: 'You haven't given me your
phone number.'

The door slammed behind him. The manager frowned.
Susan ignored his disapproval and moved into the window
to get a better view. She could see Bergerac dodging
through the traffic, apparently oblivious of the blaring
horns and screeching brakes around him. A tall man
carrying a briefcase came sprinting out of the market,
with another man in close pursuit behind him.

Bergerac swerved to cut off his flight. Their quarry
suddenly stopped, realizing that he was trapped between
the two policemen. His hand snaked into his pocket
and reappeared holding an opened flick-knife. Bergerac
moved slowly towards him, his eyes narrowed with
concentration.

The pusher's nerve broke. He dashed across the road
towards the estate agent's; Bergerac and Goddard con-
verged behind him.

His feet reached the pavement only a second before
the rest of him did: Bergerac dived forward in a flying
tackle and caught him round the knees. Caulfield's heavy
body jarred against the pavement. Goddard came in fast
behind Bergerac. He kicked the knife out of Caulfield's
hand and cuffed his wrists behind his back.

Susan found she could breathe again. She picked up
her clipboard and went outside. Bergerac was slumped
on the pavement; he was panting because the tackle had
winded him.

He glanced up at her with the ghost of a smile. 'Excuse

14

the interruption,' he gasped. 'Office number's 31821, extension 2 . . . home is 22916.'

Susan kept a straight face as she wrote down the phone numbers. 'Thanks,' she said, recapping her pen. 'I take it you'd like a nice quiet district?'

Chapter 2

Percotti fingered the blue-black stubble on his chin. He should have had a shave at Heathrow before catching the Jersey flight. He wriggled uneasily in his seat. His dark suit felt too tight and he knew he was sweating more than usual.

He knew she must still be there, but some inner compulsion drove him to make doubly sure. He turned round, allowing his eyes to roam up the length of the plane, as if he was looking for the nearest stewardess.

Arlene Roskin's burnished head was visible over the seat-backs. She had a window seat and seemed to be talking animatedly with the man beside her. The man was an old guy, and he looked like a Brit. Probably just a chance meeting, but Percotti thought he had better check it out, just in case. You didn't run unnecessary risks on this sort of operation.

He got to his feet and edged down the gangway towards the lavatories. The stewardess was moving the drinks trolley in the opposite direction, which gave Percotti a plausible reason to pause by Arlene's row.

The old guy had a tanned, cheerful face with small, shrewd eyes. There was an unlit cigar in one hand; he used it like a pointer to emphasize what he was saying. On the folding table in front of him was a large Scotch on the rocks and a portable computer keyboard. Percotti's eyes slid upwards to the rack above their heads. The flight bag must belong to the old man. The Gucci travelling bag and the briefcase were Arlene's; Percotti had noticed them at Heathrow.

He edged round the drinks trolley and continued down

to the lavatory. As he went he could hear Arlene's crisp voice: 'I work for one of the major TV networks.'

'Let me guess,' said the man beside her, twirling the ice in his glass. 'You're coming to Jersey to see one of our resident film-stars? Or our best-selling author?'

'Close.' Arlene Roskin paused. Her instinct was to say nothing. But the man was a Jersey resident and he looked well-heeled as well: he might make a useful contact if Howard Bailey proved difficult to track down. She decided to compromise. She leant marginally closer to him, allowing her breast to brush against his arm. 'I'd like to say more, but it's a bit hush-hush.'

To her relief, the man nodded understandingly. 'Aye, right,' he said. 'Well, if there's anything I can do to help, the name's Charlie Hungerford.'

'Thanks.' Arlene's eyelashes fluttered. 'I'm Arlene Roskin. Glad to meet you, Charlie.'

She allowed him to buy her a drink, and they continued talking for the rest of the flight. Hungerford told her he was a millionaire, and Arlene thought he was probably telling the truth. After all, weren't the Channel Islands a tax haven? At first she found it difficult to follow everything he said: his accent was British all right, but it wasn't like the ones you heard on the movies and on TV back home; it must be one of those regional ones.

Hungerford continued to be attentive to her after they had landed. He insisted on giving her a lift to her hotel – it was on the coast, overlooking St Aubin's Harbour. Charlie claimed it was on his way home.

Her opinion of him rose considerably at the airport: not only did his car turn out to be a Rolls-Royce, but he received a deferential salute from a uniformed policeman who addressed Hungerford as 'Deputy'.

Charlie explained, with a deprecatory shrug which did nothing to conceal his pride in the title: 'Not quite Washington. Just the Jersey Parliament, actually.' He

17

coughed modestly. 'But I hope to be a Senator quite soon.'

Neither of them noticed that Percotti was keeping them under observation. He followed them through the terminal building, mingling with the crowd as best he could. He saw Arlene getting into Hungerford's car and managed to hail a cab before the Rolls was out of sight. 'Follow that Rolls,' Percotti grunted as he climbed in. The driver's eyebrows shot up, but he said nothing.

Percotti was relieved when the Rolls swung into the forecourt of the big hotel overlooking St Aubin's harbour. He had been worried that Arlene might have gone to the man's home. An unknown private house could have caused him a lot of headaches.

A top-hatted doorman sprang forward to open the passenger door; his alacrity suggested that Hungerford was a regular and generous tipper. A young porter, not much more than a kid, came forward for the luggage. Percotti told his driver to stop in the forecourt. He rolled down the window to get a better view: yes, Arlene had nothing else with her – just the briefcase and the fancy travel bag she had kept with her on the flight.

The porter glanced towards Percotti and came up to the open window with a welcoming smile on his fresh face. 'Take your luggage, sir?' The briefcase and the travel bag were clearly neither bulky nor heavy.

Percotti shook his head. 'No thanks. I'm not staying. Cab-driver, take me on, will you?'

He sat back in his seat. As the taxi pulled out of the forecourt, Percotti looked back out of the rear window. The kid was still standing there, the bags in his hand. He looked puzzled.

Arlene unpacked methodically, keeping an eye on the time. She lunched on a sandwich in her room. She rang Directory Enquiries to see if they would give her an

18

address to go with Howard Bailey's unlisted phone number; as she had anticipated, they refused.

It was a fine afternoon and she decided to take a walk round that pretty little harbour. She left her bags in the room but locked up carefully. When she passed reception on her way out, she handed in her key and told the girl to tell any callers that she would be back in half an hour.

The forecourt was flanked by a terrace which was studded with tables and chairs. It was crowded with guests enjoying the view and the duty-free liquor. Percotti sat alone at one table, an untouched drink beside him, pretending to read *Time* magazine. He caught sight of Arlene as soon as she emerged from the hotel. His eyes followed her as she walked briskly across the forecourt towards the exit.

An amateur would have moved in right away; Percotti turned over the page and waited until a minute had slipped by. Jersey might seem a Mickey Mouse sort of place, but Percotti didn't intend to let his standards slip.

He stood up and sauntered across the forecourt and into the hotel. The pretty receptionist greeted him with a smile. Percotti pulled an envelope from his inside pocket.

'You got a Miss Roskin here?' he demanded. 'She should have checked in today.'

'I'm sorry, sir. You've just missed her.'

'That's okay.' Percotti flipped the envelope on to the counter between them. 'Will you see she gets this?'

'Certainly, sir.' The receptionist turned away and slipped the envelope into a pigeon hole. Percotti noted that a key dangled beneath it; he moved a foot to the left so he could see over the receptionist's plump shoulder. The room number was 27.

He nodded his thanks to the girl and strode purposefully away in the direction of the bar. As soon as he was sure he was out of her range of vision, he veered sharply to the right towards the bank of lifts. His luck was in: one was waiting, so he wouldn't have to hang around in the foyer.

He stabbed the button for the second floor, remembering that second floor in this godawful country meant third back home. The door whispered shut behind him and the lift moved smoothly upwards.

When the lift doors opened, Percotti saw that a wheeled linen basket was blocking his exit. The uniformed porter hastily pulled it back, muttering an apology which Percotti did not bother to acknowledge. He walked quickly round the corner of the corridor. Once he was out of the porter's sight, he fumbled in his pocket for the multi-purpose penknife he always carried. He doubted that he would need a more sophisticated tool for a hotel bedroom lock.

The young porter was still standing by the open doors of the lift. He was sure he had seen that swarthy man somewhere before – and recently. Suddenly he clicked his fingers: it was the man who had been in that taxi this morning – the one who had almost seemed to be following that American friend of Mr Hungerford's, the lady in number twenty-seven.

Behind him, round the corner of the corridor, came the soft scrape of metal on metal, followed by a click.

The porter's mind raced to put the facts together: someone had closed a door very quietly; and round that corner was room twenty-seven. Automatically, he trundled the trolley into the lift and pressed the ground-floor button. The head porter was always criticizing him for his over-vivid imagination, but there was no reason why he shouldn't have a word with Sally on reception. She might have noticed something.

He waited impatiently beside the desk. Sally was dealing with a couple of tourists who were evidently under the impression that she was an encyclopaedia on two legs. When at last the couple moved away, she looked across at him with a grin.

'What's up, Harry? You look as if you're about to burst.'

Her grin faded as Harry gabbled out his story. She told him about the man who had left the envelope for Miss Roskin and reached for the phone.

'I'd better call hotel security.'

Harry could hear the muted buzz of the phone ringing. As it rang for the fourth time without an answer, his patience snapped. He grabbed the pass-key from its hook under the desk and ran for the lifts.

The second-floor corridor was as silent as it had been when he left it. Harry walked cautiously along it. Some of his enthusiasm had already evaporated. Maybe he should let Geoff handle it: after all, security was his job.

He paused outside the door of twenty-seven. He could hear nothing inside. Perhaps the man had already left. The thought of Sally pushed him on: he didn't want to lose face in her eyes. He knocked on the door – gently, at first, and then more loudly.

There was no reply.

Harry inserted the pass-key, twisted it and pushed the door open. For an instant he stood on the threshold, gazing at the chaos. No one could say his imagination had run away with him this time. Miss Roskin's bag had been turned inside out. The drawers had been upended on to the carpet. The wardrobe gaped open, its hangers bare of clothes. The bedding had been dragged off the bed.

The door to the bathroom was open and the light was on in there. Harry moved forward a few paces. Both the bedroom and the bathroom were empty. The bloke had gone – but there was no harm in making sure. He checked behind the wardrobe door and stepped inside the bathroom.

Harry just had time to realize that the shower curtain

was moving. Something hard and sharp crashed on to his skull. The tiled floor rushed up towards him.

As he fell, he could hear someone screaming. Then the hard enamelled corner of the wash basin dug into the other side of his head.

Harry didn't feel pain. He didn't feel anything at all.

Bergerac was about to go off duty when the call came through. He had made appointments to view three flats that evening, but Barney Crozier wasn't concerned about that. The Inspector's viewpoint was typically simple: a guest at the St Aubin's Hotel had been robbed; a young porter there had been beaten unconscious by the thief; and, since the guest in question was an American tourist, it was a job for the Bureau des Etrangers – more particularly, for Jim Bergerac.

Bergerac accepted it philosophically. Never being off-duty was an occupational hazard for a policeman; that fact had been one of the reasons why his marriage foundered. It wasn't as if there was anyone waiting at home for him. Not now.

The porter was still unconscious, with DC Barry Goddard waiting patiently by his hospital bedside. So Bergerac drove first to the hotel, where he interviewed the manager and the security man. The facts of the case weren't in dispute. The porter had become suspicious about a man who wasn't a guest entering Room 27. The intruder had hidden behind the shower curtain in the bathroom and used a metal shoe rack to inflict some vicious damage on the porter. The intruder had then scooped up Miss Roskin's valuables and got away via the fire escape, just before the security man arrived on the scene. Bergerac eyed the security man's spreading girth and whisky complexion and wasn't surprised: he looked like the kind of man who was always late when there was trouble around.

A receptionist had also seen the intruder; but she wouldn't be back on duty for half an hour. Bergerac decided to interview the guest while he was waiting.

The manager ushered him up to Miss Roskin's room and introduced him. The manager's distaste for the whole affair was obvious: crime, like death, was bad for hotel business. Arlene Roskin, however, went out of her way to welcome Bergerac. As they talked, he automatically summed her up: cool and attractive, certainly – and not a hair out of place, despite the shock of violent robbery.

The preliminaries over, she looked at him with a slight frown puckering her forehead. 'I still don't understand how he did it, Sergeant.'

Bergerac showed her the envelope in his hand, angling it so she could see it was empty. 'It's an old trick. Empty envelope with your name on it – '

She caught on quickly: 'So he gets my room number – '

'*And* he knows you're out.' Bergerac gave her a rueful smile and went back to the routine questions. 'Everything's missing but your clothes?'

Arlene nodded. 'Everything. Passport, cheque book, credit cards, my briefcase with all my papers, including my air ticket.' Her mouth tightened. 'Pretty damn stupid of me to leave my purse behind. But I was only taking a stroll.'

'Money?' Bergerac asked.

'Not a lot. Three hundred dollars, plus around fifty pounds in sterling. One or two bits of jewelry. If he thought I was one of your loaded US tourists, he was mistaken.'

Bergerac looked thoughtfully at her. 'Whoever he was, he had you singled out, Miss Roskin.'

'I guess so.' Arlene Roskin obviously took the point, but she didn't like the idea; Bergerac couldn't blame her. He allowed her to change the subject: she wanted to know how Harry was.

23

While Bergerac told her, she went over to the dressing table and picked up an unopened bottle of Scotch. 'Could you use a drink?'

Bergerac shook his head. Of course he could use a drink, like any other member of Alcoholics Anonymous could use one. He was relieved when Arlene decided she wouldn't have one either.

He brought the conversation back to the robbery, eliciting the fact that only the hotel and Arlene's New York office knew she was coming to Jersey. Bergerac methodically moved on to the next question:

'Talk to anyone on the plane?'

'Well, yes,' said Arlene slowly. 'My neighbour on the flight from Heathrow. As a matter of fact, he gave me a lift here when we arrived.'

'There you are, you see.' Bergerac scented a lead. 'He might have – '

'But he wouldn't want to rob me,' Arlene burst in. 'He's a millionaire – a Mr Hungerford.'

'Charlie!' Bergerac almost groaned aloud. His ex-father-in-law knew everyone and went everywhere – which wasn't hard on an island the size of Jersey. As far as Bergerac was concerned, it wasn't an unmixed blessing.

'You know him, then?' Arlene asked.

'Like one of the family,' Bergerac admitted.

Arlene pressed home her point: 'So would he break into a hotel room?'

'No.' Bergerac shrugged. 'He's capable of a lot of things, but not that.' It was his turn to seize on a change of subject: 'Forget Charlie. A busy TV executive flies specially to Jersey. This isn't a holiday, is it?'

'Correct.' Arlene smiled. 'And perhaps you could help me, Sergeant Bergerac. I expect you know Howard Bailey? I don't mean on television.'

'I've caught a glimpse of him now and then. He's given it all up, hasn't he? Shut himself away from the world?'

24

Arlene ignored the question. 'He's the man I've come to see. Only I don't know exactly where to find him on this island. I had his phone number, but the thief took that.'

Bergerac chose his words carefully: 'And you want me to lead you to his door? I can't do that – I'm a police officer.'

She didn't try to persuade him: she was intelligent enough not to expend time and effort to no purpose. The stand-off became mutual when Bergerac asked her if the robbery could have any connection with her proposed visit to Howard Bailey. She refused to give him even an inkling of why she wanted to meet the man.

'I can't help you, Sergeant.' The smile which accompanied her words did nothing to mask her determination. 'TV's a nasty, cut-throat game. People steal ideas. My business with Howard Bailey has to remain a secret for now.'

The interview with Arlene Roskin, Bergerac admitted to himself, had got him practically nowhere. But later that evening his luck changed. For a start, Sally the receptionist could describe the suspect – in his thirties, stocky, Italian-looking and with an American accent. Harry recovered consciousness and was able to confirm the description as well as reconstruct the events of the crime. And he provided another lead: the sighting of the suspect in a taxi trailing Arlene and Hungerford. There was a strong possibility that the thief had travelled to Jersey on the same flight as Arlene Roskin.

But it was Sally who provided the real bonus when she revealed that Arlene Roskin had deposited a cassette in the hotel safe when she checked in. Now why hadn't she mentioned that? Bergerac persuaded Sally to let him hear the tape. Sure, it wasn't exactly orthodox police procedure, but sometimes you had to cut corners.

The tape explained a great deal about Arlene's passion for secrecy. If Tony Abellini was in a talkative mood again, Arlene Roskin wasn't afraid of rival TV networks.

She was afraid of the Mafia.

Chapter 3

The following day began badly for Bergerac, and it looked like that was how it was going to stay.

He woke up, half an hour later than usual and with a thick head. Life could give you hangovers, almost as easily as alcohol. The first thought which swam sluggishly into his consciousness made him feel even worse: the case he was on might have a Mafia angle.

Then, to cap it all, he remembered that today was the department's moving-day. The Bureau des Etrangers was returning to the fold.

Since its establishment nearly four years ago as an independent department to handle crimes relating to outsiders on the island, the Bureau had occupied its own building in St Helier's Royal Square. Its pleasant Georgian façade contrasted sharply with the warren of jerry-built rabbit-hutches inside. Bergerac liked it – and he also liked the fact that the department could operate without the rest of the Jersey States Police hanging around its neck.

But several senior officers in the force had opposed the Bureau's semi-autonomy from the start. They had lobbied unceasingly, both within the force and among the politicians. The bureaucratic centralists had finally won the day on the grounds of economy: the lease on the Royal Square building had come up for renewal, and the company which held the freehold was asking more this time round.

Bergerac drove to the main police headquarters where the Bureau's new offices were located. As he parked in the courtyard, he was briefly cheered by the sight of

Caulfield being shepherded into a Jersey prison van by two uniformed policemen. But his mood dropped sharply once he got inside the building. Barney Crozier was giving the assembled staff a pep-talk about the wonderful advantages of the new arrangement. At first it puzzled Bergerac, because the loss of autonomy caused by the move couldn't help but make a dent in Crozier's personal empire.

That problem was solved when he heard some sycophant congratulating Crozier on being made up to Chief Inspector.

'Oh, I get it,' Bergerac muttered to Barry Goddard. 'A proposal of marriage: Barney accepts, gets promoted and brings along a demoted Bureau as his dowry.'

Barry nodded glumly. There was a chuckle from Charlotte, the plump secretary who, in Bergerac's opinion, did more to keep the Bureau running efficiently than anyone else. Certainly a damn sight more than Crozier did.

Crozier's promotion was particularly bitter to Jim, though he tried to persuade himself that it was ridiculous to have sour grapes about it. Four years ago, he and Barney had both been detective sergeants, and both candidates for the golden ladder of accelerated promotion. Now Crozier had made it – while Bergerac had been left where he was.

Bergerac's lips twisted. It was the alcohol which had made the difference – that and the crushed leg. He was lucky to be in the force still. He shook his head: no, it wasn't the alcohol's fault. Allowing yourself to think that was almost as much a crutch as alcohol itself had been. He could only blame himself for losing the promotion race – not Crozier, nor the booze. Barney Crozier could make the right moves to the right people: he was a classic example of Organization Man. Bergerac, on the other hand, was as out of place in office politics as Henry VIII

28

would have been in a monastery. The fact that he was a bloody-minded loner was the real reason why he was still a DS.

But for how long? Crozier's promotion meant they might be intending to push someone up to Inspector in his place.

Bergerac pushed the thought away and began to go through his mail. The only item of interest was a large envelope addressed to 'Sergeant Jim'. Inside was an irrepressibly vulgar card, inviting him to the Gala Reopening of the *Fin de Siècle* nightclub in St Helier. The card featured a glossy photograph of Diamante Lil, the new co-owner. The nightclub had also acquired a new name – Lil's Place. Lil had recently sold the Royal Barge and was trying to make the move from publand to clubland. Everyone seemed to be moving these days.

Diamante Lil – the flamboyant *nom de guerre* concealed a real name of breathtaking ordinariness – was one of Bergerac's closest friends. She had been one of the few who had stood by him when the crash came four years ago. He hoped she hadn't bitten off more than she could chew with this new venture; the police had been compelled to close down the *Fin de Siècle* twice, under its previous ownership. He flipped over the card and chuckled as he read the message which she had scribbled on the back:

Do come tonight, Jim. Don't bother to bring handcuffs and truncheons. We have all those sort of things in the cabaret.

A shadow fell across his desk. Bergerac looked up to see Crozier standing over him, with the usual frown on his forehead. Bergerac had always thought that stony face had missed its vocation: it should have belonged to a hanging judge.

Crozier dispensed with polite preliminaries. 'I just had

Charlie Hungerford on the phone. What are we doing about the hotel robbery?'

'What's it to him?'

'Miss Roskin's a friend of his, apparently. Now that Charlie's on the Law-and-Order Committee – '

'*Charlie!*' Bergerac fought back a temptation to laugh. 'My God – two shock appointments in one day.' There was a suppressed titter from Barry Goddard's corner, and Bergerac realized that he hadn't been altogether tactful. 'Oh . . . well done on your step-up, Barney. You really are in the fast lane.'

'Technically the committee has purely advisory status.' Crozier paused. 'But you know what Charlie's like. She had drinks at his house last night, just after you saw her. She's an "important American visitor" – that's a quote.'

It was as near to a plea for help as a man like Crozier would ever get. Bergerac swiftly outlined the course of his investigations so far. As he talked, his mind was elsewhere, calculating the probabilities. Arlene Roskin wasn't the sort to let the grass grow under her feet. Her priority was not the robbery but Howard Bailey's address. That would have been her real reason for visiting Charlie. If Hungerford hadn't told her, then someone else would have done – Deborah, Bergerac's ex-wife, perhaps; or even Jerome O'Brien, the middle-aged playboy who was Deborah's latest boyfriend.

The source of the information was irrelevant, of course. But it was a moral certainty that Arlene Roskin was spending this morning laying siege to Bailey's fortress-like mansion overlooking Huguenot Bay. Bergerac smiled to himself. He'd be prepared to bet that a woman like that would manage to breach the defences before lunch.

'What have *you* got to grin about?' Crozier demanded. 'I don't want sweetness and light in this office. I want results.'

* * *

In point of fact, Arlene Roskin had penetrated the defences in comfortable time for elevenses.

Directly after breakfast, she had hired a car and driven out to Huguenot Bay. Bailey's house was easy to find: it was perched on the cliffs overlooking the small bay. Not that it was easy to see the house itself – it was protected by a wall which was never less than eight feet high, and usually more like ten. It was topped with a blend of ancient and modern technologies – broken glass and an electronic alarm system. There was an entry-phone beside the massive gates.

Howard Bailey was clearly obsessed with privacy. Arlene pulled up on the other side of the road and waited. There was no point in making a frontal attack.

She hadn't long to wait before her opportunity arrived, in the shape of a van belonging to a firm of garden furniture suppliers. The van-driver identified himself over the entry-phone; the gates swung slowly inwards; and Arlene drove through them, bumper-to-bumper with the van.

Bailey was furious, of course. He came striding across from the poolside terrace where the swimming-pool was. Beside the pool, a rowing machine glinted in the sun. He was wearing a faded towelling robe and had a deep tan.

For an instant, Arlene wondered if she had come to the wrong place. Bailey had changed since he had last appeared on television. It wasn't just the obvious things, like the beard and the longer hair. He seemed indefinably scruffier and less imposing – it was almost as if he was a physically smaller man. As he came closer, she saw that his face was far more lined than it used to be. *Not quite so boyish*, she thought. *Wonder if he's still got the charm?*

When she introduced herself, his face became bleaker than ever. He told her again that he had no intention of taking up her offer. Arlene appeared to accept his refusal. By now the housekeeper had joined the delivery man in

31

their audience. Arlene played on Bailey's typically British dislike of making a scene in public in order to get herself invited in for coffee. He showed her into his study. Once they were in private, it was an easy matter to persuade Bailey at least to listen to the tape she had brought. Whatever his views on making a comeback, he couldn't help being curious about the contents of the tape.

Mrs Wallace, the housekeeper, brought them coffee. As they sipped it, Abellini's gravelly voice filled the room. '. . . I hope you get this tape okay. It's a piece of dynamite – mind how you handle it. And for God's sake watch your step, old buddy. Keep it to yourself. I'm waiting to hear from you . . .'

Arlene had no need to listen closely: by now she knew it practically by heart. She stared alternately at her host and at the book-lined room where they sat. At the other end, away from the comfortable easy chairs, was a large worktable holding a word processor. There were a number of TV awards whose remarkable ugliness was no doubt counterbalanced by the prestige they conferred. Photographs were everywhere – perched on the book-shelves, on side tables and on the walls. Most of them showed Bailey on intimate terms with the famous. President Carter looked as if he was being victimized by him; Mrs Gandhi looked inscrutable; Castro was blowing cigar smoke at him; and Bob Hope was looking as if he was pretending to be Bob Hope. Arlene looked at one photograph for longer than the others. Bailey was standing at the top of an imposing flight of steps beside an obese black man who was wearing a highly ornamental uniform. The black man was beaming at the camera, showing a perfect range of capped teeth. Bailey looked as if he had seen a ghost.

Abellini's voice was replaced by the hiss of blank tape. Arlene leant forward and switched off the machine.

'It's all right,' she said, guessing the likely trend of his thoughts. 'There's been complete security. Just me and two senior guys at the network know about this.'

'That's as may be.' Bailey shook his head, as if to clear it. 'Some more coffee?'

'No thanks. Well?'

Bailey gestured at the array of photographs. 'It's no good. I can't do it. I've left all this behind.' He sounded almost wistful. 'You know the reason.'

'The President Jamulla incident?'

'Yes.' He glanced at the photograph of himself with the fat African. 'I swore, you see. After him, there would be no more interviews. That's how it's been, and that's how it'll stay. Living here quietly in Jersey has meant a great deal to me. I'm a changed man – I'm clear of the rat race and, above all, I'm still sane, whereas once I thought I was going mad. Only it was the world that was going mad.'

It was a speech which would have sounded pompous if someone else had said it. But Bailey ended it with that famous, self-deprecating smile which stripped the pretensions from the words and revealed the determination beneath.

Arlene knew defeat when she saw it. She also knew that the loss of a battle was not the same as the loss of a war.

They chatted for several minutes more. She stressed that the offer remained open, but didn't press it. He asked if he could keep the tape. She agreed, of course: it was addressed to him and in any case she had made several copies.

When Bailey showed her out, he took her through the conservatory adjoining the study. It was more like a museum than a place for growing plants. Bailey used it to display his collection of antique games. The haunted expression had gone from his face: in its place was the almost religious glow of a collector in his holy of holies.

Behind him, Arlene frowned: she should have been briefed about this.

She manufactured an appropriate enthusiasm and made a point of taking a closer look. Some she recognized – among them a delicately inlaid Syrian backgammon board, Chinese Chequers, Mah-Jong, bagatelle, a pre-war table football and a set of intricately painted skittles.

Bailey paused beside an exquisite racing game: brightly-polished silver horses stood motionless above green baize lanes. '*Cheval*,' he said proudly. 'Nineteenth century French. Place your bets . . .' He turned the handle at the side and the horses cantered round a circuit of the track. 'And this' – he turned to a set of letters in a walnut box inlaid with brass – 'is Queen Anne. It's a form of Scrabble – they say she invented it.'

'Look,' Arlene said, emboldened by the happiness on his face, 'before I go back, let me take you out to dinner? You're not that much of a recluse, are you?'

Bailey looked at her for a moment and suddenly smiled. He reached over and picked up an invitation card from the nearby shelf. Arlene caught a glimpse of someone who looked like a brothel madame and of the words *Lil's Place*.

'I've a better idea,' he said.

As Bergerac drove up the cliff road towards Bailey's house, he was passed by Arlene, going in the opposite direction. She didn't notice him, but he certainly recognized her; he had been expecting that their paths would cross, somewhere along the line.

Another car passed him, a couple of hundred yards after Arlene's. Bergerac caught a fleeting glimpse of the driver – of a swarthy face above a dark suit. For an instant he wondered if it could be the same man who had done the hotel job. He dismissed the idea almost immediately: there were thousands of swarthy-skinned people on Jersey, many of them immigrant workers. Paranoia was another occupational hazard of his job, especially on a cast like this; it was all too easy to get into the state of mind where every other person you saw looked like a mafioso.

Bailey showed no surprise when Bergerac arrived – after Arlene's visit, he seemed to be expecting the police. He led Bergerac into his study. The first thing Bergerac noticed was the tape on the corner of the desk.

'Arlene said you were investigating the theft.'

Bergerac pointed to the tape: 'At least that wasn't stolen.'

Bailey glanced warily at his guest. 'She told you about the tape?'

'No, but I listened to it just the same.' Bergerac could see that Bailey was about to protest, but he gave him no time to do so. 'I'm a copper, okay? I'm just trying to piece this thing together.' He outlined his reasons for suspecting that there might be a Mafia connection with the hotel theft, and warned Bailey that he, as well as Arlene, could be in danger.

'Seems hard to imagine, here in Jersey.' Bailey's voice sharpened. 'How could they get on to it so fast?'

'Abellini put the finger on some of their really top people, didn't he?'

'I'll say he did!' Bailey paused, searching his memory. 'It started when Tony's son, Alberto, was killed in a Las Vegas double-cross. His son was everything to him, so when he decided on revenge he didn't just sing – it was a whole bloody opera which reverberated around the whole of the States. He named names of the Mafia bosses and their rackets in five major cities. The FBI made their biggest round-up for years. The ripples spread wide, even back to Italy. Abellini's a number one target.'

'Will you interview him again?'

Bailey shook his head. 'Not likely – not even for that crock of gold they're offering.'

Bergerac decided to try another approach. 'I had a look in our files,' he said casually. 'When you left London to live in Jersey a year ago, we were advised by Scotland Yard that there had been a threat on your life.'

Bailey shrugged. 'TV celebrities get plenty of those.'

'The file says the threat was connected with a programme you made on an African dictator.' Bergerac nodded almost imperceptibly towards the photograph of Bailey and President Jamulla.

'My last interview. But I fail to see – '

The buzz of the telephone interrupted Bailey. He picked up the receiver and almost immediately passed it to Bergerac.

It was Charlotte, calling from police headquarters. 'Sorry to disturb you, Jim. But Inspector – sorry, *Chief* Inspector – Crozier thought you ought to know that the American woman's things have been recovered. Found dumped on a beach – and empty.'

Bergerac thanked her and rang off. He looked across at Bailey. 'Miss Roskin's going to be travelling light.'

Chapter 4

Bergerac reached the St Aubin's Hotel just after lunch. Arlene Roskin was out, but he decided to wait. He needed her to identify her belongings. Quite apart from that, it was time that she realized that she might have worse enemies to deal with than rival networks. He bought a newspaper and settled down at a coffee table in the corner of the foyer.

She arrived twenty minutes later, looking as immaculately self-possessed as ever. She was carrying a bulky canvas bag and headed straight over to the reception without looking in Bergerac's direction.

Bergerac folded his newspaper, got to his feet and followed her. He recognized that sort of bag – banks issued them to those of their customers who habitually paid in large amounts of cash. He bent his head so he could read the lettering on the side: THIRD INTERNATIONAL.

He knew the name: it was one of the many American banks which found it worth its while to maintain a branch in Jersey. As he drew nearer the desk, he could hear Arlene telling the receptionist to put the bag into the safe. The receptionist asked if she wanted a receipt.

'I most certainly do,' said Arlene grimly. 'There's one hundred thousand pounds there. Check it if you like.'

'You want police protection with an amount like that,' Bergerac said quietly behind her.

She turned abruptly, smiling with mechanical charm when she recognized Bergerac. When she had her receipt, they walked across to the coffee table where she identified her belongings.

'You got the son of a bitch who hurt that kid?' Arlene asked.

Bergerac shook his head. 'Not yet.'

Arlene shot him a shrewd glance. 'Could have skipped the island, huh?'

'Somehow I don't think so.'

'How do you figure that out?'

'Let's start with the money in the safe.' Once again, Bergerac checked that no one in the foyer was near enough to overhear their conversation. 'Every man has his price, right?'

Arlene's face hardened. 'What the hell are you talking about?'

'Tempting Howard Bailey into a comeback.'

'That's hardly police business,' she snapped.

'He threw you out.' Bergerac sounded faintly bored, as if he was reading a statement in court. 'And I doubt if the cash will lure him. But never mind television. You could be risking your neck – you know that?'

'Heaven sakes, *why*?'

'You might as well know – I had a listen to Abellini's tape here. Before you saw Bailey.'

'You bastard.' Anger wiped the attractiveness from Arlene's features. 'That's not legal.'

Bergerac sighed. 'All in the line of duty. I've warned Bailey, and I'm warning you. It may not be simple theft: there may be Mafia in this.'

'The soul of discretion, huh?' Arlene spat. She stood up, forcing Bergerac to look up to her. 'Well, get this straight, Sergeant. I'm trying to bring off the most important deal of my career. And I'm not going to lose it because of the fanciful suspicions of a bunch of rustic cops. So stick to your routine job and stay out of the television business.'

She walked briskly away towards the lifts. If she'd been the sort of woman who flounced, Bergerac thought, now's the time she would do it. He watched the lift doors close behind her. That self-control was formidable; Arlene's temper had really flared up, but never once had she raised her voice.

Four hours later, Bergerac was wondering about another woman's self-control. This time his interest was personal, not professional.

It was well after normal office hours, but Susan Young seemed as helpful and as friendly as ever, as she unlocked the front door of the third flat they had seen this evening. It was not as if he was a tax exile, the class of client for which Jersey estate agents usually reserved their preferential treatment.

The flat was in a newish block above St Aubin's Bay. A small hall led into a large sitting-room which seemed even more spacious than it was because of the absence of furniture. There were picture windows which gave on to a balcony. Bergerac crossed the room and stared out over the sea. A view like this would be some compensation for having to leave the Vineyard.

He followed Susan into the kitchen. 'It needs a little work,' she said, pointing to the eye-level cupboard which sagged drunkenly over the sink. It was one of the things he liked about her: she hadn't tried to give him the hard sell.

They walked through the rest of the flat, with Bergerac trying hard to concentrate on where he was rather than whom he was with.

When they returned to the sitting-room, Bergerac wandered back to the view.

'Apart from the kitchen,' Susan said behind him, 'the rest is in fairly good decorative order. And it's a very sunny flat.'

Bergerac turned round. 'How far would the vendor come down?'

Susan spread out her hands. 'A couple of thousand, maybe.'

'Still a bit out of my reach.' Bergerac unlocked the catch and slid back the window.

'You could try an offer,' Susan said as she followed him on to the balcony.

They leant side by side on the rail of the balcony. For the moment, both were content to say nothing. The tidal harbour below them, enclosed by its two jetties, was crowded with small yachts and cruisers. A few hundred yards offshore was the bulk of St Aubin's Fort. It had been built by Henry VIII, and had once protected the privateers which flourished in St Aubin. It had always shocked Bergerac to realize that, within the lifetime of his parents, that fort had been part of Hitler's Atlantic Wall.

His eyes moved back inland and he abruptly forgot history. He had a good view of the forecourt of the St Aubin's Hotel, and the sports car parked by the main entrance immediately caught his attention. He had seen it – or one precisely like it – parked in Howard Bailey's drive this morning. As he watched, the man himself came out of the hotel, accompanied by Arlene Roskin.

Bergerac's lips pursed in a silent whistle. 'Well, well. She doesn't give up easy. No wonder she's a vice-president.'

Bailey opened the car door for Arlene. She was wearing a long dress, and Bailey looked considerably smarter than he had been this morning. A few seconds later, the car roared into the main road. An evening out, Bergerac thought. He remembered that he had seen one of Diamante Lil's invitations lying on Bailey's desk, not far from the tape.

'Vice-president?' said Susan, looking puzzled. 'Who?'

Bergerac pretended he hadn't heard the question. He looked back at the flat behind him. 'Nicest of the ones

40

you've shown me over. Pity it's the most expensive. It might have been different if I'd heard they'd made me Inspector.'

'There are two others to see,' Susan reminded him.

'Office hours are long gone.'

'I don't mind.' She sounded as if she meant it.

Bergerac grinned. 'Hard to please, aren't I? Tell you what: let's skip the viewing for tonight. Fancy a free champagne supper?'

Diamante Lil reckoned she had about fifteen seconds to feel smug in, before duty called again. And she thought she might as well enjoy it while she could, because the way things were going duty was going to be calling until well into the early hours.

She sipped at the glass of champagne which the barman had put at her elbow and gazed across the nightclub. She knew it was a Gala Night, but she hadn't expected *Lil's Place* to become so crowded so quickly. Most of the tables were full now, and the floorshow area was already packed with dancers, bobbing to the music of the band.

Many of the faces were familiar, of course, and a pleasing proportion of them were both wealthy and influential. A lot of them had been loyal customers at the Royal Barge. There was even a sprinkling of celebrities, including ones like Howard Bailey who were rarely sighted in St Helier itself. Bailey was talking to that American he had brought – a woman to whom Lil had taken an instant dislike. She prided herself on her intuition, and that Arlene Roskin looked like a piranha who happened to be dressed by Dior. Still, perhaps she was famous too – and celebrities were always good for business. She made a mental note to mention Arlene to the publicity photographer.

Finally, she stole a look at herself in the mirror behind the bar. She was pleased with her appearance tonight:

her dress outshimmered every other woman's in the club. She chuckled to herself: *Diamante by name and Diamante by nature*.

Jean-Luc, her senior waiter, emerged from the side door to the left of the bar. On his tray was a gleaming ice bucket. Lil sighed: duty had called.

She beckoned Jean-Luc to her and quickly checked the label on the champagne bottle. Jean-Luc was reliable, but you had to make sure these little touches were exactly right. She nodded approvingly when she saw he'd brought out the Dom Perignon '73.

The two of them expertly picked their way through the crowded club, with Lil distributing smiles and pats on the arm without lingering to talk. They reached a table in the centre of the front row. Jean-Luc set down his tray with a flourish and effortlessly uncorked the bottle.

'There you are, Charlie.' Lil smiled seductively at Hungerford. 'For you, a special vintage.'

Hungerford glanced quickly at the bottle's label and smiled. He was a man who enjoyed the grosser forms of flattery. 'Bless you, Lil. This thrash must be setting you back a bit.'

'Not so much me as my principal backer – Alain Lambert.'

'Oh aye?' A note of respect crept into Hungerford's voice. 'The Frenchman who runs the Brittany Casinos Group?'

Lil nodded. 'There's a rumour the Jersey gambling laws might change one day soon. If so, we'll turn this into the first casino.'

Jean-Luc poured two glasses.

Hungerford raised his heavy eyebrows. 'I hope you aren't trying to bribe me as a member of our Parliament?'

Lil clinked her glass against his. 'Now would I do a thing like that, Charlie?'

A flurry of new guests caught her eye and she left

him soon afterwards. She was delighted to see that Jim Bergerac was among them – and even more delighted that he was accompanied by a very pretty girl.

'Jim! Glad you could make it.'

Bergerac smiled back. 'Well, you know it wasn't for the free booze. But this is Susan Young – and she *does* drink champagne.'

Lil showed them to the table she had kept for Bergerac. She chatted to Susan as they crossed the club, with Bergerac following behind. The band's number came to an end, and the dancers streamed back to their tables. Bergerac was not altogether surprised to find himself confronted with his blonde and beautiful ex-wife.

Both of them paused in the middle of the crowd. Jerome O'Brien, Deborah's escort, hadn't noticed the meeting; he continued in the direction of Hungerford's table. Neither Susan nor Lil realized that Bergerac was no longer following them. For a moment he and Deborah were isolated among the swirl of guests.

'Hello, Debs.' He kicked himself for sounding defensive; somehow he often did with her.

'A new girlfriend?' Deborah was eyeing Susan's retreating back. She looked at Bergerac, her eyebrows twitching upwards. 'She's pretty.'

'A new boyfriend?' Bergerac nodded towards Jerome O'Brien, instantly taking an irrational but powerful dislike to the Irishman's slightly shopworn good looks. 'He's pretty.'

Deborah gave him the sort of look which reminded him why they got divorced. Without another word she made off in the direction of her father and Jerome. She was definitely flouncing, Bergerac thought; she lacked Arlene Roskin's inhibitions.

He rejoined Susan. Jean-Luc brought champagne for her and orange juice for Bergerac.

'Who was that you were talking to?' she asked when the waiter had gone.

'My ex-wife, Deborah.'

Susan glanced over her shoulder at Hungerford's table. 'There's a strong whiff of money from that direction.'

'I suppose estate agents can tell?'

'In fact this place reeks of the stuff.' Susan gestured with her glass towards a table at the end of their row. 'The man we saw from the balcony, with the lady you called a "vice-president": he's over there. I remember who he is now: Howard Bailey. We sold Bailey his house last year.'

Bergerac pretended not to notice Susan's barely concealed curiosity. 'I'm in good company, then.'

She was about to say more when there was a long drum roll from the band, followed by a crashing chord. Most of the guests stopped talking and looked expectantly towards the stage. Lil appeared at the microphone on cue, picked out by a spotlight. Her husky voice came over the PA system:

'Ladies and gentlemen, I hope you're all enjoying yourselves. There are no speeches tonight, except to thank you for coming. It's lovely to see so many well-known faces – well-known at the Royal Barge, I mean – and I hope it'll be the first of many occasions in this club. But now it's cabaret time – and it gives me great pleasure to introduce the first of the several fine artistes we have to entertain you. Will you give a big welcome to the local girl with the silver voice who made us all so proud in the Eurovision Song Contest. Ladies and gentlemen – Harriet Lejeune!'

The club lights dimmed. The band went into the lush introduction of a ballad. Lil passed the microphone to a slim girl with an engaging smile. When Harriet began to sing, a series of lingering beach-shots was back-projected on to the screen behind her. There was a murmur of

44

appreciation from the guests, partly because of Harriet's singing, and partly because the beaches in question were Jersey ones. Appropriately enough, Harriet's lyrics frequently mentioned the word 'home'.

The problems began just after the second chorus of the song.

First, the back-projection faltered. Then the screen went blank. Harriet and the band must have realized that something was wrong behind them, because of the change in the light; but, being professionals, they continued without missing a note.

Lil, standing at the back of the club with Jean-Luc, swore softly. 'I might've known that screen gadget would play up.'

Jean-Luc touched her elbow. 'Look, it's okay – it's working again.'

Her relief was shortlived. The screen lit up again, but the images it showed were completely different. The colour quality had changed: it was faded, almost bleached, as if the film had been over-exposed.

The content of the images contrasted bleakly with the saccharine sentimentality of Harriet's ballad. The film had apparently been shot in the garden of a large, colonial-style mansion. The building's stucco was crumbling, and the garden clearly hadn't seen a gardener for some time. Heavy tyres had churned up the lawn, and the snout-like shape of an armoured personnel carrier could be seen in the rear of the shot. A dozen heavily-armed Africans wearing crisply-laundered combat fatigues were lashing three men to stakes in what looked as if it might once have been a lawn-tennis court. The captives – two whites, one black and all young – were naked except for olive-green trousers. Their faces were dark with stubble and blood. The camera zoomed in to show the weals which criss-crossed their torsos and the crushed flesh where their fingernails had been. Worst of all, it showed the captives' eyes; the big screen magnified the blank despair in them.

The soldiers formed up in a line, their mouths wide with silent laughter. An officer called them to order. The camera cut away to show a portly African regarding the scene with benign approval.

The images changed with bewildering frequency: twelve Armalites, levelled at the prisoners; the officer's mouth opening with a word of command; red blotches appearing on the three captives; the bodies slumping against the stakes; and the portly African's capped teeth, revealed by a smile of child-like pleasure.

The screen went blank.

By this time the nightclub was in an uproar. The murmurs of consternation had grown steadily louder among the guests. Harriet and the band had abandoned the ballad in the middle of a chorus and were now staring with fascinated horror at the screen. When the execution took place, a shudder ran through the entire club; several women shrieked.

Lil came out of her trance as the film ended. She pushed aside Jean-Luc's restraining arm and darted out into the hall. She was conscious only of an immense anger: someone had dared to sabotage *her* Gala Evening. She ignored the indignant cries behind her and ran, as fast as her dress would allow, down the corridor which led to the back-stage area.

She flung open the door marked *Lighting Control* and burst into the dimly lit control room beyond.

'*Dan!*' she yelled.

But the club's technician wasn't there. She moved a step forward and gasped. She could see a body on the floor, half-concealed by the table on which the video and film-projection equipment stood.

Suddenly she felt a powerful shove in the small of her back. She sprawled forwards, tripping over the motionless

46

legs on the floor. She realized belatedly that they must belong to Dan.

Behind her, the door slammed.

The Gala Evening had swiftly turned into a catastrophe.

Twenty minutes later, at least half the guests had gone, many of them making angry comments about jokes in the worst of taste. For the remainder, the sparkle had gone out of the occasion.

Bergerac escorted Lil down the corridor towards the control room. Barry Goddard, who had arrived a few minutes before, followed them. Lil was still shaking – she wasn't physically hurt but the shock had been considerable.

'Did you notice Howard Bailey's gone?' Bergerac said. 'He looked very badly shaken.'

'I'm not surprised!' Lil's tone was tart. The shock might be receding, but her anger certainly wasn't.

'You didn't see who pushed you?'

Lil shook her head wearily. 'But Dan caught a reflection of him in his projection window.'

Dan was waiting for them in the control room. He was slumped in his chair, massaging his head where the blow had caught him. The electrician wasn't a young man, and he was still groggy. Bergerac had already phoned for an ambulance. But his head had cleared enough for him to answer questions.

'I thought he was one of the club acts,' he told the two policemen. 'They often come in to check a light cue. He was dark and seemed well-dressed. Difficult to tell, but I'd say he was in his thirties.'

'Same bloke who did the hotel job?' Goddard muttered to Bergerac.

Bergerac shrugged. 'Same rough stuff.'

'Yeah.' Goddard's face brightened. 'Well, we finally got the airport taxi-driver. He's outside – and he knows where to find him.'

Chapter 5

'If Charlie Hungerford pokes his nose into police business again like that, a complaint goes straight into Parliament.' Crozier breathed heavily through his nose. 'From the top.'

Bergerac tossed the file back on Charlotte's desk. 'I thought I'd better warn you. An unsolved robbery and two assaults – it's a gift for him now he's on the Law-and-Order Committee. Police incompetence is just the ticket for a rising politician.'

His voice was bitter. Charlie had tried to pump him for information about the case, earlier this morning. It was typical of Hungerford to avoid the proper channels in the hope of personal advantage. He probably planned to flex his political muscle at the Committee meeting this afternoon, and astonish his colleagues with his inside knowledge.

Crozier scowled. 'If only you'd managed an arrest last night.'

'That was bad luck, not incompetence,' Bergerac snapped. He continued in a quieter voice: 'The taxi-driver took me and Barry to Perkins' hotel on the Havre des Pas. Perkins – if that's his real name – must have been on the balcony and recognized the taxi-driver. While we were going up, Perkins was coming down – using the balconies as a ladder. He got away in the taxi – the driver had left his keys in the ignition. We eventually found the taxi abandoned near the bus station.'

'That doesn't alter the end-result: we're getting nowhere. Have you talked to Arlene Roskin this morning?'

'I tried to. She'd just checked out before I phoned.' Bergerac paused. 'She took her piggy-bank out of the hotel safe.'

'Presumably she's taking the money back to the bank. I imagine Howard Bailey's even less likely to take up the offer than he was before.'

Bergerac nodded. 'I spoke to him an hour ago. He's scared. Came to Jersey to get away from it all. First the American dame turns up, and now it seems he's being leaned on from another direction.'

'Is he willing to give us any help?'

'No. Seeing that Jamulla programme he made really threw him. Apparently Miss Roskin's network swore it had been destroyed. Every single foot of it. It must have been a hell of a shock, having it shown in front of that audience. All he wants to do now is speak no evil, see no evil and hear no evil.'

Crozier frowned. 'Put a discreet watch on his house.'

'Right.'

'With the Bureau's new set-up here, we have to be even more on our toes.' Crozier walked away towards his office.

Bergerac looked after him. 'Yes, sir, *Chief* Inspector,' he muttered. Crozier seemed to be more interested in pleasing his superiors than in solving the crime.

Charlotte caught Bergerac's eye and grinned.

'Jim?'

Barry Goddard burst through the swing doors. He had several sheets of computer print-out in his hand.

'I checked the incoming planes two days ago.' He spread out the top sheet on Charlotte's desk and jabbed a finger at one of the names. 'Here's our Mr Perkins, on the eleven-ten from Heathrow. And there's Arlene Roskin on the seat-plan, next to Hungerford.'

'So Perkins did follow her to Jersey?' Charlotte said.

'Yeah, but there's more than that. I got the airline

49

computers to take us further back, on transatlantic flights. And guess what? Perkins sat right beside Miss Roskin all the way from New York to London.'

Bergerac looked up sharply, his mind racing to deal with this latest piece of information. It was as if the case was a kaleidoscope: someone had shaken it, changing its pattern entirely.

'One more thing,' Barry added quietly. 'Their bookings were made by the same Manhattan travel agent.'

The big white cruiser from Cherbourg was moored at one of the pontoons in the new marina. The oil-stained water, gleaming in the midday sun, slapped gently against the fibre-glass hull. It was a luxurious craft, with twin engines and more electronic technology than most people could afford in their houses.

A casual observer would have assumed that a boatload of wealthy French people had popped over to Jersey for a day of shopping and tourism. But only one of the four on board was French; and none of them had the slightest interest in the sights and shops of St Helier.

Marcel, the skipper, was on deck, ostensibly splicing a rope and actually acting as a sentry. He was a *pied noir* who had lost his family, his home and his scruples during Algeria's bloody struggle for independence. He had also acquired two long scars across his rib-cage and a great many paramilitary skills.

Technically, the boat belonged to him. But ownership was dependent on the observation of certain conditions. The most important of these was that Joe Conte and his colleagues took precedence over all other customers. It was surprising how often a Manhattan-based organization could find a use for a powerful boat in the English Channel.

There was a murmur of voices in the main cabin below, but Marcel was too far away to hear what they were saying. He was only mildly curious about what was going on; as long as the money was right, he didn't really care. And this trip should be lucrative, if nothing else. When Conte had phoned from New York last night to set up the rendezvous, he had ordered Marcel to bring a selection of hand-guns. Guns and profitability, in Marcel's experience, invariably went together.

A huge yawn caught him unawares. He had had no sleep last night and wished he could afford to take a nap in the sun. He pulled out a crumpled packet of untipped Caporals from his breast pocket and lit up. Conte must be feeling the strain as well, though he showed no visible sign of fatigue and was as impeccably turned out as usual. He had taken an overnight flight from New York to Heathrow, and then flown on to Jersey. He'd arrived at the marina at ten o'clock, only a couple of hours after Marcel.

The other two had come later. Marcel hadn't met them before, but he'd immediately categorized them as muscle man and iron lady. Unlike Conte, they had both taken care to reach the cruiser as unobtrusively as possible.

The talking below in the cabin grew louder. It sounded like muscle man was having a hard time. Marcel could distinguish a few sentences:

'Okay, so I cracked a couple of heads – what else could I do? Anyhow, I pulled that stunt with the film. That club screen was a gift! It wasn't easy, and it was just for a few minutes. But it made one hell of an impact.'

Joe Conte held up a warning hand, and Percotti subsided into silence. When the conversation resumed, it was too low for Marcel to hear.

'The fact remains, Dino, that all your activity has achieved very little.' Conte's voice was dry and unemotional. 'Fix us all a drink, would you?' He looked at Arlene, who was sitting opposite him. 'And how did you get on?'

Arlene shrugged. 'I didn't. I told you it wouldn't work, Joe. Money doesn't count with our famous TV personality.' She patted the cash-bag on the seat beside her.

Conte nodded towards the bag. 'We'll need some of that to pay our French connection for the use of this floating gin-palace.'

'Why hire a boat?' Arlene asked.

'Because as soon as we're through we'll want to get clean away from this island.' Conte scowled at Percotti. 'Dino's heavy methods have made that necessary, if nothing else.'

'Hey!' Percotti protested. The drinks he was carrying wobbled dangerously. 'I just did what you asked me. No other way. It was easier for her – and she didn't score.'

'You shut up, dummy,' Arlene snapped.

Percotti flushed. 'Listen, nobody calls me that and – '

'All right, all right,' Conte said wearily. 'Cool it, both of you. We got work to do.'

'I just don't like him.' Arlene spoke as if Percotti was elsewhere. 'He gives me the creeps. His breath smelled on the plane trip.'

'I said cut it out. You don't choose who you operate with.' He took the drink which Percotti held out to him and sipped it slowly. 'Now, let's figure it out. Howard Bailey won't do the interview and he won't take the money. So he won't contact Abellini. But we do know how to get to Bailey with that African film. So now it's different tactics.'

'Have you thought about my idea?' Arlene interrupted.

Conte nodded slowly. 'Yeah. It's a good one – which is just as well as it's the only one we've got right now. Dino, get Marcel in here.'

A few seconds later, Marcel followed Percotti into the cabin. He scratched the stubble on his chin. 'You want to talk about money now?'

'Later. First we got a job for you. It's a little out of your usual line, but you'll get a bonus. Arlene, you tell him.'

She leant forward and spoke slowly and clearly to Marcel. 'You phone Howard Bailey and explain you're a French antique dealer visiting Jersey. You've heard he's crazy about old games, and you happen to have one on offer. It's a Russian game from the days of the Czar – a nursery carousel. He'll find it irresistible.'

Marcel grunted. 'It seems simple enough. And what happens then?'

Conte gestured with his glass towards the locker where Marcel had concealed the hand-guns. 'Then we all go see Mr Bailey.' He chuckled, and raised the glass to Arlene. 'No wonder you made vice-president.'

The manager's office was cube-shaped; the fittings all seemed to be made of chrome and leather. The room looked as if it had been designed as a set for one of the more expensive American soap operas.

The manager himself, however, was English – a small, balding man with a conservative suit and the trace of a West Country burr in his voice. There were sharp, vertical worry-lines on his forehead.

Bergerac introduced himself and explained his reason for his visit to the Third International's Jersey branch. The banker called for the relevant file but showed the traditional professional reluctance about disclosing its contents. His worry-lines became deeper.

It was easy enough to understand why, Bergerac thought. Reticence was a built-in feature of the man's job. On the other hand, the manager of an offshore bank would have no wish wantonly to offend the Bureau des Etrangers. It was not impossible that the bank would one day need the Bureau's cooperation.

53

Bergerac sighed and decided to use the old ploy of feeding a little information in the hope of getting more.

'The theft of all her credentials was obviously rigged. I just checked with the American TV company – they've never heard of a Miss Arlene Roskin.'

The banker pursed his lips as if Bergerac had said something in bad taste. 'I know nothing about that, you understand.'

'Yet she drew a hundred thousand pounds in cash from this bank – yesterday, wasn't it?'

'Correct.'

'So where did it come from?' Bergerac demanded.

The manager fiddled with the lapel of his jacket. 'We have to be – ah – *ultra*-discreet about the sources of foreign money.'

'This is different,' Bergerac pointed out. 'It could be a criminal matter.'

The older man shrugged and picked up the file from the side-table near his desk. He studied it for a moment, while Bergerac restrained his impatience.

'The funds were made available from New York,' he said at last. 'They came from the account of a trading company – Alfa International of Brooklyn.'

Bergerac's face relaxed. 'That sounds more like it.'

'Like what?' The manager's voice was pettish.

'Mafia money.'

The banker shot a startled glance across his desk. Then his training reasserted itself. 'Really?' he said coldly. 'Money is just money as far as we're concerned.'

'Of course,' Bergerac said smoothly. As far as he was concerned, money lay at the heart of a good proportion of the cases he had to deal with.

'However.' The manager referred back to the file and relented slightly. 'There's one thing I can tell you. You've got her name slightly wrong. She produced her passport, you see, for verification of identity. And the name wasn't

Roskin: it was Rosconne.' He paused, looking blandly at his visitor. 'That's Italian, isn't it?'

Bergerac stood up. 'Thank you, sir. You've been very helpful.' He had an uneasy feeling that the manager had known the direction his enquiries were tending, right from the start.

He left the bank and walked back to where he had left the car. As his hand touched the doorhandle, a thought occurred to him. *The passport.* He should have noticed that point before; he should have checked with the bank about Arlene's means of identification as soon as he had heard about the withdrawal. No bank would hand over a hundred thousand quid without convincing evidence of the bearer's identity. And Arlene wouldn't have had time to get a substitute passport from the US consulate.

So she must have retained her passport, claiming it had been stolen with the rest of her things. He could have caught her up on that small discrepancy, if he had been a little more alert – and a little more suspicious. He slid into the car and fired the engine. It would be something to remember the next time he was feeling conceited about his abilities as a detective.

He drove quickly to the police headquarters on Rouge Bouillon. He took the stairs two at a time. Crozier looked up as Bergerac came into his office.

The Chief Inspector greeted Bergerac's report with a frown. 'So she was Mafia all the time?'

'The whole thing was a fix – designed to fool Howard Bailey.'

'And us,' said Crozier drily. 'What about Abellini's tape message?'

'My guess is that's a fake as well – cobbled together from old interviews.' There was a bleak expression on his face. Last year, someone had pulled a similar trick on him. It had nearly cost him his job – and started him drinking again.

Crozier nodded; his eyes avoided Bergerac's. That tape had fooled him as well.

'The point is,' Bergerac continued, 'Bailey knows where Abellini is, and that's what they wanted. That's – '

Charlotte burst into the office without knocking, her face tense. 'Excuse me, sir. Constable Goddard's radioing in.'

Crozier switched on the desktop receiver and lifted the microphone. 'Crozier.'

'Car drew up a moment ago, sir,' Goddard said. He was keeping his voice low, and they had to strain to hear it over the static. 'Three blokes and a woman.'

'What does she look like?' Crozier snapped.

'White, slim build, about five-ten, well-dressed, blonde or light-brown – '

'All right,' Crozier interrupted. 'Could be Miss Rosconne?' he said to Bergerac.

'It is,' he replied curtly. Who else did Crozier imagine it could be?

Goddard's voice came tinnily through the loudspeaker. 'One of the blokes is getting out. He's at the speaker-grille by the gates . . . must be calling up the house . . . he's getting back in the car. I don't know what he said, but Bailey's let them in.'

'Right.' Crozier was already on his feet, edging around his desk. 'We're on our way.'

Chapter 6

Bailey came out of the house on to the terrace and walked quickly along the edge of the pool towards the drive-way. His thin face was alive with interest. If Monsieur Mercier had been telling the truth about the nursery carousel, it should be both authentic and in good condition. Its acquisition might be some compensation for the unpleasantness yesterday. Some – not much.

He turned his mind resolutely away from the memory. He had been reading up about carousels since Mercier's phone call. If he was really lucky, this example might be one of those manufactured for the celebrated St Petersburg toymakers, Stein and Maclaren, whose customers had included the imperial nursery. If he was luckier still, Mercier might not know the true value of what he was selling.

As he came round the corner of the house, Bailey stopped abruptly. Arlene Roskin, his *bête noire* of the moment, was standing on the gravel. Behind her were three men whom he had never seen before. His first thought was that the network had sent in reinforcements. Then another thought occurred to him.

'What's this?' he said. The professional in him noticed that his voice was slightly unsteady.

The oldest of the three men stepped forward. 'We want a word, Mr Bailey.'

'Sorry, Howard.' Arlene's synthetic smile flitted across her face. 'Let me introduce you. This is Joe Conte.' She indicated the other two men. 'And Dino Percotti and Marcel.'

The names and Conte's accent told their own story.

57

Bailey swallowed. 'No need to explain who they are. *And* you?'

Arlene shrugged. ''Fraid so.'

Bailey's eyes flickered from one face to another. When he spoke again, his voice was firmer. 'I congratulate you. Very convincing.'

'It wasn't too difficult,' Arlene said. 'I used to work at another network.'

Conte cleared his throat. The preliminaries were over. 'You see, Mr Bailey, if you'd just agreed to do the interview, you'd have taken us to Tony Abellini.' He paused before adding: 'Now we must try to persuade you some other way.'

Bailey backed away. 'You won't find Tony through me.'

Percotti, at a nod from Conte, began to saunter round the pool, peering into the different rooms of the house. Conte turned back to Bailey.

'Are you alone?'

There was no time to answer.

'Mr Bailey?'

A middle-aged woman with a helmet of grey permed hair appeared at the far end of the terrace.

'Do you want me first thing in the morning, or could I – '

Her voice died away as she saw the guns which appeared in the hands of the four visitors.

'It's all right, Mrs Wallace,' Bailey said quickly. 'This is my housekeeper,' he explained to Conte. 'She's just leaving – she has children to collect.'

The last five words were in the nature of a plea on humanitarian grounds; but Conte did not belong to a philanthropic organization. He jerked his thumb towards the house. 'Both of you. Inside.' Percotti and Marcel moved closer, underlining the futility of protest.

Arlene led them into the conservatory. Conte stared at the games. 'Very nice,' he said mildly. 'Very dinky.'

Percotti seized the handle at the side of the *Cheval* and gave it a rough twist. When Bailey protested, he lifted the game and dropped it on to the tiled floor. Bailey's face crumpled as he looked at the wreckage of wood, twisted metal and baize.

'Where did you recruit this meathead?' Arlene demanded. It was not the gesture which offended her – merely the unnecessary destruction of a valuable antique.

Conte didn't reply. He waved the Walther PK, indicating that Bailey should precede him into the study.

Bailey and Mrs Wallace were told to sit down – and effectively immobilized by the big armchairs. Percotti and Marcel covered the doors, their eyes watchful. Conte prowled around the room, apparently absorbed in the trophies and photographs.

'Be sensible,' Arlene said softly to Bailey. 'Does it really matter to you whether they get Abellini or not?'

'I won't shop him. He's a brave man. *Is* he dying, by the way?'

Arlene sighed. 'He was just as ruthless as anyone else in the brotherhood.'

Joe's leisurely circuit of the room had brought him behind Bailey's chair. 'Bravery means a lot to you, Mr Bailey?' He moved round so Bailey could see him. 'I mean, you wouldn't like the world to know the truth about you, right?'

Bailey's face tightened, but he said nothing.

Conte moved with a speed and violence which contrasted sharply with his previous actions. He ripped down the photograph of President Jamulla and Bailey and held it inches away from the latter's eyes. 'I hear you sweated when Dino ran the film clip of this. Why don't we enjoy the rest of the nauseating story?'

Arlene switched on the television and the video, inserting an unlabelled cassette which she took from her handbag. The screen flickered. A series of unedited shots followed. The jumbled sequences and the absence of a soundtrack gave the film a surreal quality.

It began with a number of location shots, showing an African city which seemed to be gripped simultaneously by war and famine. Only the soldiers were plump. Then, once again, Bailey recognized the ruined garden of the presidential palace. Tremors ran through him as the execution of the three mercenaries was replayed.

Conte added his own commentary. 'He laid on the firing squad for you, didn't he? And you did nothing to stop it.'

'How could I?' Bailey said hoarsely. He was condemned to ask himself that question for the rest of his life; and he knew he would never find an answer.

His eyes were still hypnotized by the screen of the television. As he watched, his younger self appeared, talking with the camera crew.

'You didn't try, did you?' Conte continued. 'You didn't even order your own camera man to stop. The great television hero, the celebrated man of the people – too scared for his own skin. There you are again. Take a good look.'

Bailey was with Jamulla now. The President was pointing at the mercenaries and making some jocular comment. Bailey had managed no reply other than a weak, propitiatory smile.

'Three young mercenaries put to death for your entertainment.' Conte looked curiously at Bailey. 'The parents of one of those white boys threatened to kill you, they say. That right?'

When the executed men slumped backwards against their stakes, Bailey's nerve cracked, both on the screen and in real life. On screen, he covered his eyes and began to retch.

In the present, he tried to get to his feet. 'Stop it, will you!' he cried hoarsely.

Conte smiled. He reached over and switched off the video. This was a cat-and-mouse game, Bailey realized: and he was the mouse.

'Tell us where to find Tony,' Conte said, 'and the film is yours. Otherwise there are plenty of muck-rakers who'd love to have it. They'd make it much more public than last night. Why, even your Queen who gave you the OBE might see it.'

Bailey, who had slumped back in the armchair, lifted his head. 'No,' he said defiantly. 'You can do what you like with the film.' He avoided the eyes of Mrs Wallace; he had seen the disgust on her face as she watched her employer's last interview.

Conte looked faintly bored. 'In that case, you give us no alternative but to use other methods.'

In the silence which followed, Bailey felt his defiance ebbing away; despair flooded back in its place.

Suddenly the answer-phone on the desk buzzed. Someone was at the gate.

'Answer it!' Conte snapped to Mrs Wallace. 'Be natural.'

The housekeeper gave him a frightened look and picked up the phone. Percotti moved smoothly to her side and buried the muzzle of his automatic in the iron-grey curls above her ear.

'Sergeant Bergerac to see Mr Bailey.'

Conte covered the phone receiver with his hand. 'Make him go away,' he hissed.

Mrs Wallace swallowed. 'I'm afraid that's not possible,' she told Bergerac. 'He – he's not here.'

'When do you expect him back?'

'I've no idea,' she replied, her eyes on Conte. 'He didn't say. Is there a message?'

'No. Just let him know I called by.'

There was a click as Mrs Wallace replaced the receiver on its rest. She crumpled against the desk. Conte ignored her.

'Dino. Marcel,' he ordered. 'Go check if the cop's gone.'

Percotti slipped through the conservatory on to the terrace, with Marcel close behind him. They picked their way across the garden as if it were a potential minefield. There was an aluminium ladder propped against the wall, probably left there by someone pruning the climbing plants which clung to the old bricks. Percotti motioned to Marcel to hold the ladder steady against the wall. He climbed slowly, making sure that the soles of his shoes didn't rattle against the metal rungs. Inch by inch, he raised his head above the level of the wall, taking care not to break the circuit of the alarm system.

His body stiffened as his eyes took in what was happening in the road below. There were three cars out there – a squad car, an unmarked saloon and the stupid two-seater job which that clown Bergerac drove. Men were milling around the cars: he could see a couple of uniformed cops conferring with three plainclothesmen, one of whom was Bergerac. He couldn't make out whether they were armed. Surely British cops didn't carry guns?

He turned his head sharply as he caught movement on the edge of his range of vision. Two more uniformed men were getting out of the saloon, and these two were definitely armed. They carried rifles with telescopic sights.

Percotti raised his gun instinctively, resting the barrel between two pieces of broken glass on the top of the wall.

He squeezed the trigger.

* * *

The knot of men dissolved in an instant, as everyone took cover behind the cars. The marksmen had seen the blur of movement at the top of the wall before Percotti fired: they were able to fling themselves sideways. One of them rolled and came up in a kneeling position in the lee of the Triumph Roadster; he had time to squeeze off a return shot, but the bullet ricocheted off the wall and whined harmlessly away.

Crozier shouted: 'To hell with that alarm – get over the wall!'

Percotti's head had vanished. Bergerac and the two marksmen were on to the wall in seconds. Bergerac loosed off a round from his Smith and Wesson, but the two fleeing figures ahead continued running and disappeared into the house.

He jumped down from the wall and, covered by the marksmen, tugged open the heavy gates. The harsh clangour of the alarm erupted from the house. Crozier, Goddard and the two other policemen edged through the gates.

'We can't rush the house,' Bergerac told Crozier. 'Not with Bailey and the housekeeper in there.'

Crozier nodded. 'Right. Everyone fan out and take cover.'

Behind them they could hear the sirens of police reinforcements coming up the cliff road. From the house came the tinkle of glass from upstairs windows.

Bergerac's eyes narrowed as he concentrated. All of them would be upstairs by now, he guessed; these men were pros. They were breaking windows to clear their lines of fire. Probably they were using the furniture to build barricades. They would only need to have two fields of fire – that way they could prevent the police from working round to the back of the house.

More armed police were deploying round the garden. One of the new arrivals handed Crozier a loud-hailer.

63

Bergerac began to edge his way towards the Chief Inspector.

'This is the police! Listen carefully.' The amplification distorted and flattened Crozier's voice, making it sound as if it were produced by a microchip. 'The house is surrounded, and you are outnumbered. A good many of us are armed. You can't escape. Before anyone gets hurt, I suggest you surrender – '

A ragged fusillade of shots from the house interrupted Crozier's standard scene-of-the-siege speech. Bergerac noticed with interest that only one man was firing from the smaller window on the left, but at least two were using the larger window on the right.

'Now *you* listen!' The hoarse shout came from the larger window. Bergerac caught a glimpse of a middle-aged man: probably the boss. 'We have two hostages here. You try anything and the woman gets it first. You got that?'

Bergerac wriggled nearer to Crozier. 'Ask them what the deal is.'

Crozier was already raising the loud-hailer. 'What do you want?'

'That's more like it,' came the voice from the house. 'If you let us reach our car, we take only Bailey with us. Nobody stops us, okay, and nobody gets hurt.'

'Let them do that, Barney,' Bergerac muttered, 'and Howard Bailey's as good as dead.'

Crozier met Bergerac's eyes for an instant and then spoke into the loud-hailer. 'All right, we'll think about it. I have to get higher authority. You'll have to wait.'

He thumbed off the loud-hailer's switch and turned to Bergerac, his eyebrows raised in a question. The crisis had briefly dissolved the differences in rank and temperament between the two men. Once again they were working as a team, as they had when they were constables on the beat together.

'I think we could work our way under cover of that shrubbery to the back, if you gave us a diversion. Then we could get inside through the kitchen door.'

Crozier considered the idea for a moment and then shook his head. 'Too risky. Anyhow, they'll be covering the stairs. If only we knew more about the layout of the house.'

Bergerac paused. Suddenly he clicked his fingers. 'Maybe there's someone who does. Listen, Barney, can you stall the bloke in there for a while?' He leant closer and whispered in Crozier's ear.

A few seconds later, Bergerac slipped out of the garden. In the road, police cars huddled round the incident van like chicks round a mother hen. He commandeered one of the squad cars; when you were in a hurry in afternoon traffic, the Triumph was not the best car to use.

He drove to St Helier at a speed which only someone who had learned to drive on these roads could have hoped to match. He pulled into Halkett Place and parked opposite the covered market.

In the estate agent's, Susan was standing by her desk listening to a sturdy lady in tweeds who was holding forth about the number of bathrooms she considered to be a bare minimum. Bergerac strode over and grabbed Susan by the arm.

'Police,' he said curtly, cutting off the lady in mid-flow. He drew Susan aside.

She giggled. 'Lady Hopkins probably thinks you're arresting me.' Her face grew serious as she took in his expression. 'What is it, Jim?'

'Howard Bailey bought his house through you, didn't he? Did you do a video?'

Susan nodded. 'But I'm not sure it's still on file.' She opened a cupboard and ran her finger along the spines of the cassettes inside. 'Why do you want to know?'

Bergerac bent closer to her. 'Don't tell your colleagues, but we have a siege on our hands at Bailey's place.'

'We're in luck.' Susan pulled out a cassette and slotted it into the video. Bergerac, dimly aware of Lady Hopkins clucking in the background, watched intently.

The video followed the standard pattern – shots of the exterior, followed by the interior from bottom to top. At the time, the house had been empty of furniture.

Bergerac gave a grunt of satisfaction as he recognized the window on the stairs. That was where they had one of their men. The larger window belonged to the main bedroom – almost certainly they were using that as their headquarters.

'Go back a bit,' he said. 'Let's see the kitchen again.'

Susan rewound the tape. When she pressed the play button she found she had overshot: they were in the wine cellar again.

Bergerac touched her arm. 'Hold it there. What's that cupboard in the corner?'

'It isn't a cupboard – it's a dumb-waiter shaft. It starts in the cellar, rises into the kitchen, and goes on to the upstairs landing.'

Bergerac asked a few more questions and then abruptly left the shop. Susan stared after him, wondering if he ever found time to be a human being as well as a policeman. It would be nice to find out. She turned to face the wrath of Lady Hopkins.

When Bergerac got back to the house in Huguenot Bay, he found that the situation had hardly changed in his absence.

But Crozier's face looked even more worried than before as Bergerac made his report. 'I can't hold them much longer, Jim. They're threatening to come out with both hostages and force the issue.'

'Give me another five or ten minutes, Barney.'

Bergerac, Barry Goddard and one of the marksmen

slipped through the shrubbery. Crozier distracted the attention of the people in the house, by pretending that his superiors needed more information before coming to a decision.

Once out of sight of the two windows, Bergerac took a chance: he broke cover and sprinted directly for the kitchen door. He was relieved to find it was unlocked: even professionals could make mistakes sometimes.

The marksman stayed in the kitchen on guard, while Bergerac and Goddard went down to the wine cellar. Bergerac, gun in hand, squeezed into the dumb-waiter. He gave Goddard a nod, and the latter began to haul the rope which controlled the lift.

The dumb-waiter ascended with agonizing slowness. Bergerac tried not to think what would happen if the rope broke under the unaccustomed strain. He wondered when the lift had last been used, let alone serviced. The faint creaks above his head might be audible to the man on guard on the landing. He had never liked enclosed spaces at the best of times.

On one side of his prison, a rectangle of thin light lines appeared: they must be passing through the kitchen. Bergerac watched the light disappear with regret; any kind of light was better than none.

After a dark eternity, a second rectangle slid down the side of the dumb-waiter. The lift bumped gently to a stop. Bergerac forced himself to wait; he counted slowly to twenty-five. Unwelcome possibilities flooded into his mind: the door might be bolted on the outside; the hinges might screech; the guard might be looking directly at the door.

Twenty-five.

Bergerac pushed gently on the door. Just in time he realized it was one of those retractable-ball catches: he managed to hold it with his fingertip, preventing it from clicking back. Inch by inch, he eased the door open.

Light poured in. The first thing he saw were the luxuriant fronds of a Swiss Cheese plant which was obviously aiming for inclusion in the Guinness Book of Records. The plant was two feet away from him – and it stood directly in line between the dumb-waiter and the window at the head of the stairs.

The silhouette of a thickset man was outlined by the afternoon light pouring through the window. Bergerac slipped out of the lift and glanced quickly round the landing. The door to the main bedroom was a few inches ajar.

He tiptoed over the deep-pile of the carpet, eyes and ears straining to catch any sign of movement around him. The man at the window began to turn when Bergerac was eighteen inches away from him, perhaps alerted by the displacement of the air.

But he was a fraction too late. Bergerac clubbed him with the Smith and Wesson, just above the left ear. He grabbed the man as he fell, and lowered him noiselessly to the carpet.

Goddard and the marksman came quietly and quickly up the stairs.

'What was that? Go check it out, Dino.'

Bergerac froze. The voice came from the main bedroom – and so, presumably, would Dino. He nodded to Goddard and the marksman. It was time for the frontal approach.

As Percotti came through the door, Goddard jammed his pistol into his ribs with one hand and slammed the American against the door-frame with the other. Bergerac pushed past them into the room, followed by the marksman.

'Drop your guns,' he ordered.

Arlene obeyed. But Conte leapt sideways with surprising agility and imprisoned Mrs Wallace with his arm. She began to struggle, but stopped when Conte brought the gun to her head.

'Let her go,' Bergerac said.

Conte looked contemptuously at him. 'I'm walking out of here with her. So get out of my way.'

Bergerac slowly lowered his gun. Conte and Mrs Wallace, locked together in a parody of a loving embrace, sidled awkwardly towards the door. Arlene moved back to let them pass; her face was bitter, because Conte was so clearly unconcerned about the safety of any of his colleagues; the marksman's rifle was still levelled at her stomach.

Bailey hesitated and then stepped back. Conte's eyes were on Bergerac; Bergerac was trying not to make it obvious that he was watching Bailey.

Bailey's step back had brought him beside a small table near the head of the bed. On it was a lamp with a heavy china base – a graceful shepherdess with swirling skirts and slender legs. Bailey's hand, shielded by his body from Conte, curled round the waist of the shepherdess.

As Conte drew level with him, Bailey swung the lamp in an arc, rising towards Conte's head. Conte reacted immediately: he dodged sideways and down, dragging Mrs Wallace with him. As the blow failed to connect, Bailey fell forwards off-balance. Conte fired. Bailey spun round and fell, with a look of surprise on his face.

At that moment, Bergerac sprang.

He grabbed the wrist of Conte's gun-hand and bent it round behind his back. Conte let go of Mrs Wallace and lunged, with his fingers splayed, at Bergerac's eyes. Bergerac jerked away and chopped at the junction between Conte's neck and shoulder.

There was a dry, but perfectly audible crack as the collar-bone broke. The Walther thudded on to the floor. Bergerac scooped it up.

He crossed to the window to signal to Crozier; his eyes met Arlene's on the way.

'Con yourself out of this one, Miss Rosconne,' he said evenly.

The next half-hour was a blur, as far as Bergerac was concerned. It was always the same on a case like this, when the tension suddenly broke and the adrenalin seeped away from him. What he really wanted was a stiff drink; a nice cup of tea just didn't have the same appeal. He thought briefly of Susan, of the way she had smiled up at him when he snatched her away from the dragon in the estate agent's this afternoon. He wanted very much to take her where police work couldn't intrude. It would make a pleasant change for both of them.

Percotti, Conte, Arlene and Marcel were handcuffed and led away. The medical team attended to Bailey: fortunately, Conte's bullet had only nicked his upper arm. The lamp, however, was shattered beyond repair. As one of the medics came out of the study, he paused to talk to Jim.

'Funny bloke in there.' He indicated Bailey with a nod of his head. 'He wouldn't let us put his arm in a sling until he had torn up a photograph.'

'Did you see what it was?' Bergerac asked.

'Yeah. Him and some black guy with a lot of medals on his chest. Some people are *weird*.'

Bailey appeared on the doorstep just as Crozier and Bergerac were about to go.

'Excuse me,' Bergerac said to Crozier with exaggerated politeness; now the siege was over, they were back to Chief Inspector and Sergeant again. He walked across the gravel to Bailey. 'You okay?'

Bailey nodded. 'I'll be fine – only a graze.'

Bergerac looked thoughtfully at him. Something about the man's face had altered. Suddenly it clicked: Bailey no longer had his haunted look.

'Thanks for your help in there.' Bergerac paused. 'That was a very brave move you made.'

Bailey smiled. 'Thank *you*, Sergeant.'

Chapter 7

Both the Caulfield case and the Abellini case involved a lot of paperwork and court appearances – two aspects of his job which Bergerac disliked. But there was one compensation: for the next few weeks he was working uncharacteristically regular hours. In consequence he saw a great deal of Susan Young.

The friendship between them rapidly became something more. Bergerac realized just how far they had come when, one night at *Lil's Place*, he was bemoaning the fact that he would have to be out of the Vineyard by the end of the month. Since he had so far failed to find a flat he both liked and could afford, he would have to look around for somewhere he could rent for the time being.

Susan stared into the depths of the elaborate cocktail which Jean-Luc had prepared for her. 'You could always move into my place for a time. It's quite a big house. I – I've often thought of advertising for a lodger.'

'I'd like that.' Bergerac paused. 'If you're sure – '

She looked quickly at him and then away. 'Yes, I'm sure.' There was a faint stress on the *I*.

And that was the problem, Bergerac realized. She was ready to commit herself, but he was still hesitating on the edge. There were too many ghosts in his past – like the memory of his marriage to Deborah. They had married too young, of course, but that fact alone wasn't enough to explain the bitterness which had so quickly soured the relationship. The fault had probably been his: as a copper he was a natural loner, and maybe the same was true of him as a person.

Nevertheless, he needed somewhere to live – and he

wanted to be with Susan. He made plans to move in, promising himself it was only a temporary measure. It couldn't be long before he found the right place to buy – especially with the advantage of having access to inside information about the market.

It would have been so much easier to buy if his salary had been just that little bit larger. But promotion to inspector still showed no sign of coming his way. Barney Crozier was still running the Bureau, despite the fact he now had other responsibilities. He had even been given a personal secretary, Peggy, to mark his new importance. Crozier's outside interests meant that a certain amount of his work now devolved on Bergerac, as senior sergeant. It was a pity that none of the kudos came his way as well.

Despite the problems, Bergerac was in a cheerful mood as he drove into the courtyard at police headquarters on the first Monday in July. He and Susan had had a good weekend. Furthermore, he had finally tied up the paperwork on the Abellini case.

He was whistling softly as he walked into the office. He nodded to Goddard and made his way over to his desk. As usual his in-tray held a mountain of files, while his out-tray was empty. He picked up a note torn from a scratch-pad on top of the in-tray. It was in Peggy's prim, upright hand, and told him that a George Barton had telephoned.

Bergerac couldn't place the name. At that moment, Peggy herself came into the office with a file for Goddard. Bergerac tapped the note as she passed him.

'Who's George Barton?'

'He rang about an hour ago.' Peggy pursed her lips. 'Something about animal rights.'

Bergerac frowned. 'Why me?'

'He said he'd been given your name by Charlie Hungerford.' Peggy gave him a nod and moved away.

Bergerac's cheerfulness vanished. Charlie Hungerford

was becoming insufferable. Not only was he on the Law-and-Order Committee, but he had managed to get himself voted chairman a couple of weeks back. That, of course, had reinforced his delusion that he had *carte blanche* to interfere in police affairs.

The telephone on Bergerac's desk buzzed twice. He picked it up. 'Bureau des Etrangers.'

'Is that the police?' It was a woman's voice – low-pitched, attractive and with a distinct French accent.

'Well, yes,' Bergerac said.

'They killed Jerry Bruce.'

Oh God, not another nutter. Aloud he said: 'I'm sorry?'

'They killed Jerry Bruce,' the voice repeated. There was a sharp intake of breath. 'His death was no accident.'

The phone went dead. Bergerac rubbed his nose thoughtfully. Probably a nutter, but he had better check it out. Crozier had just come in and was taking off his coat. Bergerac went across and asked him if he had heard of a Jerry Bruce.

'I've heard of him.' Crozier turned to hang up his coat. 'And I wish we knew who he was. What's your interest in him?'

'I just got this funny phone call – '

Crozier smiled sardonically. 'You should be used to those.' He left the office and walked down the corridor towards the cafeteria. Bergerac followed him.

'It was a woman,' he said to Crozier's retreating back. 'Some anonymous weirdo. She said *They killed Jerry Bruce* and rang off.'

Crozier stopped and looked impassively at Bergerac. 'A man named Jerry Bruce was knocked down by a car yesterday. He died in hospital early this morning.'

'Hit and run job, was it?' Bergerac asked.

'Anything but. The car was a Rolls. Just the driver in it – a professional chauffeur named Gary Carter. Carter said Bruce just ran into the middle of the road as he was coming round a bend. He put Bruce in the back of the Rolls and drove him straight to hospital.'

'And what state was he in? Carter, I mean.'

'Fine.' Crozier shrugged and continued down the corridor. 'Well, shaken up, of course – who wouldn't be? But stone cold sober. There's no reason to doubt his story.'

They had reached the cafeteria. Crozier ordered two coffees.

'So what's the problem?' Bergerac persisted.

'The coroner isn't happy. He's not prepared to let anyone bury Bruce until he's had the answers to a couple of questions.'

The woman behind the counter set down two cups of coffee with a jerk; the contents of one of them slopped into its saucer. Crozier picked up the other one.

'For starters,' he continued, 'who the hell *was* Bruce anyway?' He patted his pocket. 'You got any change? I seem to be out.'

Typical, Bergerac thought. He handed over the money and followed Crozier back to his office. Crozier rummaged in a drawer and tossed a booklet of numbered tear-off tickets on the desk between them. Bergerac examined it: the booklet was about half-used.

Crozier took a sip of his coffee. 'That was all he had on him, except for a few quid. No cheque book, no driving licence, no credit cards – nothing. From the info on the back of the tickets, it seems he worked as a beach photographer – the kind who takes your picture whether you want him to or not, and then slips you a ticket just in case you should be unwise enough to order a copy.'

Bergerac looked up from the booklet. 'And this is the address of his studio, is it?'

'Nothing so grand. It's a holiday flat he's been renting. Apparently he came from the mainland, so it's a case for us. Or rather, for you.'

Bergerac leant forward. '*Is* there a case?'

75

'The flat was burgled yesterday, and cleared of anything that might have told us where he'd come from or who he was. At least, that's the assumption.'

Bergerac grinned at Crozier. 'Just hasn't been Jerry Bruce's week, has it?'

Dennis Dudley, the landlord of Bruce's flat, might have been taken for forty-five in bad light. Tight jeans and a grubby but resolutely boyish jersey emphasized his skinniness. But his hair was thinning and there were deep lines on his face. His eyes, around which traces of mascara could be seen, sized up Bergerac appreciatively.

'Come this way, Sergeant.' Dudley waved a limp hand towards the stairs.

Bergerac followed him up to Bruce's flat. The sitting-room was sparsely and anonymously furnished; Bruce had made little attempt to make his holiday let seem like home.

The intruders had done a very thorough job. Clothes, books and papers littered the floor. The carpet had been pulled back. The upholstery of the armchairs had been ripped open.

'It's like this in the other rooms,' Dudley said.

Bergerac bent down and examined some of the books. All of them belonged to the same subject area – the paranormal, the occult and black magic – but varied in style from the soberly scholarly to the frankly lurid. He picked up one hardback which was obviously both new and expensive. The title was *Demonkind*. The author, Bart Bellow, was one of Jersey's tax-exiles, Bergerac remembered. On the back-cover was a photograph of him. Bellow was a big man with dark eyes and heavy eyebrows. Bergerac looked up at Dudley.

'Do these books come with the flat, Mr Dudley?'

'Do you mind?' said Dudley archly. 'My interest in black magic faded when Billy Daniels did.'

'Billy who?'

'You heard, love.'

Bergerac laughed. He stood up, gesturing at the books on the floor. 'He was into the occult in a big way, your Mr Bruce?'

'Obviously.' Dudley pouted. 'Mind you, as far as I know we haven't had any virgins sacrificed up here this week. More's the pity. But how would I know? I've hardly been able to set so much as a cloven hoof in here since I gave him his keys. Jerry was what you might call a *very* private person at the best of times. And this last week – well . . .'

Bergerac obediently prompted him: 'What about this last week?'

Dudley opened his faded blue eyes to their fullest extent. 'What indeed? He'd gone like a bloody hermit crab. Hardly opened his door. I've knocked once or twice just to make sure he hadn't dropped dead or something. As it turned out, I suppose I needn't have bothered.'

They went on to the bedroom, which was even more chaotic than the living-room.

Bergerac said over his shoulder: 'You identified the body for us – right, Mr Dudley?'

Dudley sniffed. 'Yes. And they can keep that for a game of soldiers.' He gave a theatrical shudder.

'Turned you right off, did it?' Bergerac asked with a grin.

'I've seen dead bodies before.' Dudley's face was suddenly serious, and the affectation was gone from his voice. 'But I've never seen one with a look like that on his face. My God – anyone would have thought he'd just come face to face with Old Nick himself.'

'Perhaps he had.' Bergerac tried another tack. 'You live underneath, right? And you heard nothing when the flat was turned over?'

'Not a dicky-bird. Right pros, whoever they were.'

'Yes.' Bergerac picked up the Leica with its matching flash unit which was on the bedside table. It was a new model, and its retail price wouldn't leave Bergerac much change out of a month's pay. 'On the other hand, what self-respecting burglar would have left this behind?'

He pushed open the bathroom door and methodically investigated the cabinet over the basin. One bottle was unlabelled. He unscrewed the cap and poured a stream of black capsules into the palm of his hand. He looked back at Dudley, who was standing in the doorway.

'Did you know he used to take these things?'

Dudley shook his head. 'What are they?'

'Durophet.' Bergerac saw the lack of comprehension in Dudley's face and went on: 'They're anti-obesity drugs, technically. Pure speed – pep pills.'

The surprise on Dudley's face was clearly genuine. Bergerac pocketed the drugs and led the way back into the living-room. There was little more that Dudley could tell him. Bruce had paid his rent in cash and in advance; and he might have mentioned that he had come from London.

In the living-room, Bergerac trod on the corner of an upturned frame. He stooped to pick it up. It contained a photograph of a well-dressed woman in her late twenties; she had long black hair which framed a face which was very nearly beautiful.

'Who's this? His girlfriend?'

'Very much so.' Dudley smiled slyly. 'For a while, at least. Up to the end of last week she was never away from the place – day *or* night. Then all of a sudden there was no more Helene – and Jerry was doing a Howard Hughes on us. Well, I did wonder whether they'd had some sort of a row.'

'Helene, you say?' Bergerac said quickly. 'French, is she?'

'Originally, I believe. Helene Duval! – she runs this

shop in St Helier.' The moist pink tip of Dudley's tongue ran swiftly over his lips. 'From what I've heard, you'll find some even *funnier* books in there.'

Chapter 8

Bart Bellow looked at himself in the window of the bookshop. His thick lips twisted in a rare smile of approval.

The publicity photograph was slightly larger than life-size. It was the central feature of the window display. Around it were arranged fifteen copies of *Demonkind*. Bellow wondered idly how many passers-by would realize that the books discreetly outlined a pentangular figure – and how many of them would realize its significance. If they read the book, they would certainly find out.

He pushed open the door. A bell rang above his head. The bookshop was empty. There were the usual racks of brightly coloured paperbacks, the table for remainders in the centre and the major occult display along the right-hand wall. The astrology and numerology charts were new, he noticed.

Helene was near the rear of the shop, altering the display of herbs and candles on the small table to the left of the charts. She looked up as the bell rang. Bellow was pleased to see a shadow of fear pass over her face as she saw who it was. She tried to force a smile, but failed.

'Helene,' Bellow purred. 'We haven't seen you for so long – we thought you'd *died*.'

She took one step backwards, steadying herself against the table. Bellow caught and trapped her gaze.

'Well?' he said gently. 'Doesn't your favourite author at least get a cup of coffee?'

He took her arm and guided her into the small back-room of the shop. A percolator bubbled on the desk. Bellow sat down in the one comfortable chair and watched how Helene's hands trembled as she set out the cups and saucers. It was all most satisfactory.

At last he could deny himself the pleasure of probing further no longer. 'Something wrong, Helene?'

A teaspoon clattered on a saucer. Helene looked quickly at him.

'Was it really necessary to go that far?' As usual in moments of stress, her accent became more pronounced.

'Absolutely, my love.' Bellow smiled at her, and she shrank back; he pretended not to notice. 'He was dangerous to us. You were very wise to tip us off about him.'

'Couldn't you simply have warned him off?'

Bellow shook his head slowly. 'If only it could have been that simple,' he said sadly. 'But you know what *They* are like. When *They* feel insulted – ' He broke off and gave a heavy sigh. '*They* are simply incapable of half-measures, I suppose.'

The shop bell jangled. Helene got to her feet automatically, but she looked at Bellow, as if asking his permission to leave. Bellow inclined his head majestically. Helene scurried into the shop, leaving the connecting door open. Bellow's eyes followed her. He could see the rear view of a tall man; the customer seemed to be examining the occult display.

'Are you looking for anything in particular?' Helene asked.

The man turned. He had a herb jar in each hand – Dragon's Blood Balm and Templar Essence – and seemed to be finding the labels amusing.

An interesting face, Bellow thought. Rather like one of the less degenerate Roman emperors.

'A Miss Helene Duval, actually.'

Helene's shoulders tensed beneath her dress. 'I'm Helene Duval.'

'Yes, I thought you might be. I'm Sergeant Bergerac – Bureau des Etrangers. We spoke on the phone.'

'We did?'

Bellow got to his feet and moved silently towards the door.

'You said you wanted to report a murder,' Bergerac said. 'The murder of Jerry Bruce.'

'Is this some kind of joke? Jerry Bruce died in an accident.'

'That's what we thought – until you rang.'

Helene raised her voice: 'I never rang you.' Her hands clenched and unclenched themselves by her side.

'Miss Duval, you have a very distinctive accent – '

'And one perhaps that would be easy to imitate. Right?'

Bergerac shrugged. 'Why on earth would anyone want to do that?'

'Whoever rang you, Sergeant' – Helene was almost shouting now – 'it certainly wasn't me.'

'But you did know Jerry Bruce?'

'Of course. He came into the shop occasionally.'

'Oh, a bit better than that, I think.' Bergerac moved half a pace closer to her. 'He had a framed photograph of you in his flat. Tell me, why did you suddenly stop seeing him? Lovers' tiff?'

'He was not my lover. We were just – '

'Good friends?' There was no mistaking the mockery in Bergerac's voice.

Helene glared at him, but she continued to answer his questions. She claimed there had been no quarrel – it just so happened that she and Bruce hadn't seen one another in the last week or so. She had no idea where he had come from on the mainland – they had never talked about things like that.

'So what did you talk about?' Bergerac asked. 'Books?' He waved an arm towards the display. 'About the occult? Black magic? Strange encounters of the other kind?'

'Look, Sergeant,' Helene interrupted desperately. 'Why am I being asked these questions?'

'I told you. Your phone call aroused our curiosity.'

'But I tell you,' Helene wailed, 'I made no such phone call.'

'Well, put it this way, Miss Duval. Somebody did. And to me that somebody sounded a hell of a lot like you.'

Helene made no reply. After a few seconds, Bergerac nodded to her and left the shop. She moved up to the window and watched him getting into his car. Her hands continued to work, as if she was kneading invisible lumps of dough. Her face, which had been rigidly expressionless while she talked to Bergerac, crumpled. The years fell away from her and she looked like a terrified child.

There was a step behind her. She turned, her hands outstretched in a wordless gesture of supplication.

The veneer of urbanity had been stripped from Bart Bellow's face: there was brutality beneath, mixed with something still more frightening. In his right hand was a copy of *Demonkind*. She began to raise her arm.

Helene was too late. He smashed the heavy hardback across her face with all his strength. She reeled back against one of the stands. Brightly coloured paperbacks cascaded on to the floor.

Bellow put his face close to hers. He had a look of utter concentration, like a man about to make a declaration of love.

'Oh,' he said softly. 'You stupid bitch.'

Bergerac drove to the General Hospital on Gloucester Street. He parked outside Casualty – the Triumph Roadster could pretend it was an ambulance for five minutes. The receptionist glanced at his credentials and directed him down the corridor to the projection room.

Dr Frost was examining an illuminated X-ray of a diseased human lung with a certain morbid satisfaction. He was a lean, middle-aged man with a sardonic smile

83

and dark circles under his eyes. Bergerac introduced himself.

'That's what nicotine does for you.' Dr Frost snapped off the projector and extracted the plate.

'You smoke, Doctor?'

Frost snorted. 'Next question?' He picked up his bag and opened the door. Like most doctors, he gave the impression that he hadn't really got time for you because he should have been somewhere else half an hour ago.

'Jerry Bruce,' Bergerac said.

'Oh – *that* one.' Frost walked up the corridor with Bergerac in tow. 'Cause of death was heart failure.'

'Brought on by the shock of the accident, presumably?'

Frost nodded to a passing nurse and moved aside to let a trolley pass. 'Well, that couldn't have helped.'

'Did you realize he was on speed?' Bergerac asked.

'Not at the time. But the treatment would have been the same in any case.'

They had reached a flight of stairs. Frost rested his free hand on the newel post and glanced longingly upwards. Bergerac quickly produced another question.

'Did he recover consciousness at all?'

'Very briefly.' Frost anticipated the next question. 'He only said one thing.' He grinned sourly at the memory. 'It was all bloody odd, really. He objected to being sedated. We thought of course he was some kind of religious nut. Then, when I'd finally got the needle in him, he sort of fixed me with his glittering eye and said: *You've damned me.*' The doctor began to climb the stairs. He looked back at Bergerac. 'I must say that after I saw the look on the poor bastard's face, I did rather wonder. And they say you could hear the scream he gave when he died in the ward below. Maybe he knew something that we don't.'

Frost chuckled, and ran up the stairs two at a time. Bergerac watched him go, his face thoughtful. This was

84

all they needed – a case of the Hammer Horrors. Crozier was going to love this.

Bergerac had one more call to make – the mortuary. Wally, the attendant, was eating a bacon sandwich with every appearance of enjoyment. He pulled open the drawer which contained the mortal remains of Jerry Bruce. Wally's jaws continued to move. With Bergerac, he stared down at the corpse's face. He took another bite.

'Not a pretty sight,' he remarked through the bacon.

'As long as it doesn't put you off your lunch,' Bergerac replied absently.

Bruce's face was so contorted that Bergerac wondered how Dennis Dudley had been able to identify him. It was strange, the effect a fatal seizure could have on the features. No doubt there was a pedestrian medical explanation.

To the layman, however, it didn't look as if Bruce had died of a heart attack. It looked as if he had died of fear.

Bergerac noticed the man waiting in the foyer of the Bureau des Etrangers as soon as he arrived. He was a small man, in his sixties probably, though he might have been taken for younger. His features were sharp, and it looked as if he hadn't got around to shaving today.

But what set him apart was his clothes. He wore the sort of jacket that clothes designers of the 1960s had believed to be appropriate for the ideological sympathizers of Che Guevara. His mud-stained trousers had the first bell-bottoms that Bergerac had seen on a civilian for several years. His scuffed desert boots needed resoling.

The man looked up as Bergerac came through the door. He hesitated and then stood up.

'Sergeant Bergerac?'

'Yes?'

The man's lips curled, revealing yellow, irregular teeth. 'You do exist, then.' The voice was thin and harsh.

'I'm sorry?' Bergerac tried the effect of a smile. 'Have we met?'

The smile turned into a grin as a huge grey Irish wolfhound suddenly emerged from behind a nearby desk. It sniffed suspiciously and disdainfully at Bergerac. The man grabbed the dog's collar like a lifebelt. It was almost as if the touch of the wolfhound gave him moral support.

'We have met now. At last.' The man's mood communicated itself to the dog, which gave a low growl. 'No thanks to you, it seems to me.'

Bergerac looked blankly at him.

'George Barton mean anything to you?' the visitor asked.

Bergerac ignored the sarcasm in the voice. 'Mr Barton,' he said as enthusiastically as he could manage. 'I was just going to ring you.'

Barton showed his teeth again. ''*Course* you were.'

'Come on up, will you?' Bergerac led his visitor upstairs and gave him a seat. 'Now then, Mr Barton, what can we do for you?'

'For starters you can stop what's going on right next door to me.'

Bergerac concealed his impatience. He recognized Barton's type only too well: he was one of those professional fanatics who were never without a cause. Protest was his career, and the police were his natural enemies.

'And what is going on, Mr Barton?'

'Dumb animals are being tortured.' Barton waved aside Bergerac's attempt to interrupt. 'It's not even a research establishment – it's a private house.'

'What makes you think anything's going on there?'

'I don't think, Sergeant – I *know*. I've got ears. I know an animal in mortal agony when I hear it. And I've got a

86

nose, as well. I know what it is they're burning in that furnace when they're finished.'

'Look, Mr Barton, if what you're alleging is correct – '

'It *is* correct.'

'What I mean is,' Bergerac continued, 'with this sort of complaint, you have to go through the proper channels – which in this case has to be your local police.'

Barton scowled. 'I've tried that. But nobody listens. Everyone thinks I'm some kind of a nut. That's why Charlie Hungerford pointed me in your direction. Because he thought you might at least *listen* to me.'

'Of course I will, Mr Barton. But I still have to tell you that your complaint isn't any of this department's business.'

'Sergeant Bergerac! Cruelty to animals is everybody's business.' Barton's sallow face was blotched with anger. He stood up. 'Still, never mind,' he said bitterly. 'Message received and understood.'

'Look, Mr Barton – '

'*You* look, Sergeant. Look into what's going on in that house. And if you won't – well, don't be surprised if you find that there are some of us who will.'

The wolfhound's growls had grown in volume since Barton stood up. Suddenly the dog barked at Bergerac. Barton tugged him out of the office. The wolfhound stopped on the threshold and gave Bergerac a parting snarl. The dog's teeth were remarkably similar to Barton's.

Peggy, who was coming into the office as Barton was leaving, stood aside to give a wide berth to the man and the dog. She looked across the room at Bergerac.

'Another satisfied customer?'

Bergerac grinned. So Peggy had a sense of humour after all. 'I think he wanted to go walkies.'

The phone beside her rang and she picked it up. 'Bureau des Etrangers . . . Hold on, please.' She covered the phone with her hand and held it towards Bergerac. 'For you. A Miss Helene Duval.'

The first thing that Bergerac noticed was that Helene's voice sounded even more strained than before. She wanted to talk to him.

'Of course. I'll come round to the shop.'

'No – not to the shop, we're closed. Come to my flat.'

'The address?'

'It's flat four B, Jayston Tower. I'm on the top floor, facing the lift.' She stumbled over the simple directions.

'Right.' Bergerac glanced at his watch. 'I'm on my way.' He grabbed his coat and the car keys. In the doorway he almost collided with Charlie Hungerford.

'Ah, Jim.' Hungerford laid a proprietorial hand on Bergerac's arm. 'I was hoping I'd catch you.'

'Bit out of your way, aren't you, Charlie?'

'Official business, you know.' Hungerford sounded both defensive and self-important.

'With me?'

'Well, no,' Hungerford admitted. 'But – '

'In that case, I'll see you.'

Bergerac set off down the stairs. But Hungerford was not a man who gave up easily. He followed Bergerac down the stairs and along the corridor, hurrying to keep up with the younger man.

'Er – my friend George Barton – ' he began.

Bergerac stopped. 'You just missed him, Charlie – him and the Hound of the Baskervilles. Believe me, the pleasure was all yours.'

'Gave you a bit of earache, did he?' Charlie didn't sound surprised.

'I'd have thought the chairman of the Law-and-Order Committee could have channelled a complaint to the police a bit more precisely than that.' Bergerac pushed open the swing-doors which led out to the courtyard.

'He's got a right bee in his bonnet, has George,' Charlie said behind him. 'Sees vivisectionists under every bed.'

'So I gathered.' Bergerac unlocked the car and climbed in.

'So what I thought was' – there was almost a note of pleading in Charlie's voice – 'if he could get a sympathetic hearing from at least one member of the force – '

'You'd have got him off *your* back.' Bergerac started the engine.

Hungerford bent down so his head was level with Bergerac's. 'You're getting cynical in your old age, Jim,' he said reproachfully.

'I put it down to the in-laws I used to have.' Bergerac looked directly at Hungerford. 'Barton's not likely to do anything clever, is he? Is he the type to put rat poison in chocolate bars?'

'George?' Hungerford laughed. 'He wouldn't hurt a fly.'

'Possibly.' Bergerac was unconvinced. He remembered Barton's parting words to him, a few minutes ago. 'But then – with people like George – flies rate just a bit higher than people.'

He let out the clutch and drove off. Hungerford stared after him, shaking his head.

Chapter 9

Bookshops, Bergerac thought, must make more money than he'd thought they did; either that or Helene Duval had private means.

Jayston Tower was a small block of flats on the outskirts of St Helier. The flats had the sort of sea views which made a substantial difference to their price tags. The block was new, and the freeholder hadn't skimped on the furnishings of the foyer. The keynote was elegant modernity – and the elegance was so understated that it had to be expensive.

Stairs led down to the basement and up to the floors above. But the lift was waiting, so Bergerac took the easy way up to the fourth floor. He rang the bell of Helene's flat and waited. He wondered if the other flats had spyholes in their front doors.

A chain rattled; a bolt shot back; and the heavy door opened. Helene Duval had a large glass of what looked like neat whisky in her hand and a fresh purple bruise on her left cheekbone. She swayed slightly as she stood aside to let Bergerac in.

The sitting-room was large and airy. Helene sank down on the sofa and motioned to Bergerac to take one of the armchairs. She offered him a drink, but hardly seemed to notice when he declined it.

'There's something I want to clear up – about Jerry's death.' Her face twisted, as if she was screwing herself up to make a confession. 'I lied to you. We were lovers. For a while it was wonderful, but then' – she gave a wholly Gallic shrug – 'we had a row. He wanted a more permanent arrangement – to own me, to have children. I

90

couldn't accept that. There was this terrible argument. In the end, I told him I never wanted to see him again.' She looked away from Bergerac and smoothed a non-existent wrinkle from her dress. 'I suppose I got my wish, didn't I?'

'So why lie about it?' Bergerac kept his voice impersonal and low-pitched; Helene was supplying enough emotional drama for two.

'I felt so foolish,' she said with a break in her voice, 'telling the police he had been murdered. You see, when I heard he was dead, I felt he *had* been murdered – by me. Just as surely as if I'd stuck a knife in him. He kept telephoning, and I refused to take his calls.'

Helene buried her head in her hands. Her hair swung forward, curtaining her face.

Bergerac chose his words carefully: 'You aren't by any chance suggesting he threw himself in front of that car on purpose, are you?'

She shuddered. 'Please, Sergeant, don't say that. At least spare me that.'

He let the silence between them lengthen for a few seconds. 'There's nothing else you want to tell me about him?'

Helene shook her head. 'There's nothing else to tell.'

'Right.' Bergerac stood up. 'Well, thanks for your help.'

She walked with him to the front door. Bergerac looked down at the livid bruise as she held open the door.

'If I were you, I'd get a piece of steak on that.'

It took her a moment to realize what he meant. 'This?' She touched her cheek and gave an awkward laugh. 'I walked into a door.'

Bergerac stepped out into the corridor. 'You'd be amazed how many people walk into doors.' He pushed the button for the lift. 'Battered wives, usually.'

Helene closed the door behind him and leant against it

for a moment. She touched the bruise on her face, wincing at the pain. Maybe that policeman was right. And she had some steak in the fridge. But first there were other things to do.

She went back to the sitting-room and plumped up the cushions on the sofa. Underneath one of them was something she had thrust out of sight when the doorbell rang – her own copy of *Demonkind*, with a personal dedication from the author. She swallowed the rest of the whisky and picked up the phone.

A silent prayer went round and round in her head as she dialled the familiar number. *Please let him be pleased, please let him be pleased . . .* The phone went on ringing for so long that she began to hope that there wouldn't be an answer. Not that that would solve any problems in the long run.

Suddenly the ringing stopped. 'Bellow.'

'Bart – it's me, Helene.'

'What do *you* want?' Bellow snapped back.

'I – I just wanted you to know that it's all right now. I talked to him.'

'Who?' The exasperation in his voice made her shiver.

'The police sergeant – the one who came to the shop. I explained everything to him.'

'You did *what*?'

Helene hastily told him. As she spoke, she touched the photograph on the back of *Demonkind* as if it was a token of good luck.

But Bellow's voice was bleaker than ever: 'And you think he believed you? You really think he believed you?'

He slammed down the phone. Helene stared blankly at her own handset. She let it fall from her hand on to the sofa. A shiver ran through her. God, she needed another drink.

She splashed another three fingers into her glass, spilling some of it on to the cover of the book. She had failed. Deep down, that was something she had known already. And Bart knew she had failed. Probably he would have known even before she phoned. *They* would have told him.

A tear fell on to the back of her hand and shattered. Her last shred of hope was gone. *They* had a very simple way of dealing with failure.

The farmhouse itself swam into the circle of light. Its outlines hardened into focus. George Barton sighed with satisfaction. These binoculars were one of the best investments he had ever made.

The late afternoon sunlight cast long shadows over the neatly raked gravel at the front of the house. There were no cars parked there – the non-resident housekeeper had just left; Bellow had gone off somewhere half an hour earlier, in the Rolls.

Nevertheless, Barton was taking no unnecessary chances. He steadied himself between the hedge and the boundary wall which separated his land from Bellow's and scanned the façade of the house. He worked methodically from top to bottom and left to right. Each window was closed; and he could discern no movement behind them.

The contrast between this house and his own farm struck him forcibly. Bellow's roof was new, and all that fresh white paint on the outside hadn't yet lived through a winter. Barton felt anger rising through him like bile. He himself, a man who believed in freedom and the rights of all creatures, was forced to live in a slum. But a foul sadist like Bellow lived in an immaculate mansion and drove around in a Rolls. It was symptomatic of the rotten social structure of this country. He would like to tear the whole lot down and bury the faceless bureaucrats and the wealthy, selfish, privileged few whom they served deep in the rubble.

He shook his head to clear it, and forced himself to

concentrate on the matter in hand. Thinking was futile: only action was justifiable. He swung the binoculars on to the huddle of buildings behind the main house. When this was a working farm, the buildings must have been stables, barns and cow-sheds. Barton had his own theory about their present function.

Now it was time for action, he felt a curious reluctance to move. His heart-beat seemed faster and more pronounced than usual. He was sweating heavily, which was hardly surprising – he was wearing his old army surplus jacket for camouflage.

There was no point in putting it off. Every minute could be precious.

Barton put the binoculars in their leather case and laid them gently by the base of the wall. He would pick them up on the way back. They would only be an encumbrance now. He groped in his pocket for the black balaclava. Pulling it on made him feel immediately better. He was faceless now – only his eyes were uncovered. He felt he had joined all the other heroes of the people who had to wear masks when they fought their oppressors.

He scrambled over the wall, grazing his hands on the rough stone. He fell awkwardly on the other side. *I'm not so young as I was.* He picked himself up and ran across the paddock which stretched between the wall and the house. After a few yards, he stumbled. He was gasping for breath and a stitch was digging into his stomach. He staggered on.

The paddock had become huge – a green desert with no cover to shelter him. He felt strangely certain that someone was watching him, though there was no one to be seen. At one point, halfway across the field, he was sure he heard a malicious, gleeful chuckle just behind him. But when he swung round, the paddock was as empty as before.

At last he reached the nearest outbuilding. He steadied

himself against it; the warm stone was reassuring to his touch. He waited until his breathing had become less ragged and then followed the line of the building to the archway which led through to the courtyard.

The courtyard was clean and cobbled. To the left was the rear of the house. To the right and in front of him was an L-shaped range of farm-buildings. From the roof of the one nearest the house poked the gleaming aluminium cylinder of a furnace chimney. The door beneath it was heavily padlocked.

Barton looked slowly round the yard. The big barn which was parallel with the house looked like the best bet. He cut diagonally across the yard towards its door.

His footsteps were loud in that enclosed space. The sound of them bounced off the hard surfaces. At one point he thought he heard that chuckle again – but that was ridiculous: he was overwrought; his imagination was working overtime.

He lifted the heavy latch of the barn door and pushed. To his relief, the door swung silently back on well-oiled hinges. He slipped inside and immediately gasped – partly in horror, partly in relief.

Those stupid policemen were wrong – and he, George Barton, was right. The musty, unhappy smell of caged animals hit him as soon as he crossed the threshold. The light was poor – a couple of narrow slits high up in each gable – but gradually his eyes adjusted to the gloom.

The barn's interior had recently been subdivided into a series of pens and cages on either side of a gangway. Barton walked quickly along, glancing into each cage.

Dear God! There were goats, chickens, a couple of lambs, several cats – and even a pair of tortoises. What the hell was that sadist doing to them? The laboratory must be in the house itself, or possibly attached to the furnace building.

Barton shook his head. He must get his priorities right.

These creatures had to be saved. One by one he opened the cages.

The reactions of the inmates disappointed him. He had expected – well, not gratitude, exactly, but at least some sort of cooperative behaviour. The tortoises stared sleepily at him, and stayed precisely where they were. The cats came out at once, but they made a beeline for the two white rats at the end of the barn furthest from the door. The lambs walked unsteadily out into the courtyard and began to nibble the herbs which grew in carefully cultivated rows near the kitchen door. The billy-goat treated Barton as an aggressor, rather than a saviour.

Once again, he thought he heard that chuckle.

Suddenly the realization of where he was and what he was doing hit Barton. He ran out of the barn into the sunlight of the courtyard. One of the lambs raised its head to look curiously at him. He ran on, through the archway and into the paddock. The stitch savaged him and tussocks of grass made him stumble, but he ran without stopping. Only when he was over the boundary wall and safe on his own land did the panic leave him, as abruptly as it had come. He lay by the hedge, sobbing for breath, with his eyes closed.

Something warm and wet stroked his ear. He opened his eyes. The long grey face of his wolfhound stared down at him.

'Sam . . . Sam, old boy. You come to take me home?'

Barton held the farmhouse and seven acres around it on a two-year lease. The house was much smaller than Bellow's. No one had done any maintenance work on it for half a century. The roof leaked; the window frames were rotten; and the Aga generally failed to provide hot water. Dampness rose from the floor and oozed out of the walls.

The kitchen was the warmest room in the house.

Barton used it as a living-room and an office as well. Its familiar clutter calmed him immediately. He looked almost affectionately at the faded poster over the sink: it showed a cat with electrodes strapped to its brain and no front paws.

He made himself some herbal tea, choosing camomile and valerian for their soothing effects. By the time he had drunk the second cup, he was inclined to put an entirely different construction on his experiences.

He hadn't really panicked as such – he had made a rapid tactical withdrawal, as the situation demanded. He had achieved his objective through careful planning and resolute implementation. He had struck a blow for animal liberation which would certainly shake up this smug little island. The shock-waves would almost certainly reach the mainland.

The achievement deserved celebration. He opened a bottle of elderberry wine. The first sip was always a little tangy, but it was excellent by the time one reached the second glass. By the time he was on his third, he was composing newspaper headlines and deciding how he would make his report to the comrades at the next monthly meeting.

The key to Operation Noah was forward reconnaissance followed by swift, incisive action. Where the lives of our fellow creatures are at stake . . .

Before he opened the second bottle he remembered to put Sam out in the barn. Shortly afterwards, he went to bed, though it was only nine o'clock.

Sleep overwhelmed him at once. When he awoke, the bedroom was in darkness. His tongue felt double its usual size and the inside of his mouth was dry. Worst of all, he had a headache that cut into his brain like an axe.

Outside, Sam was barking – continuously, almost hysterically.

Barton groaned. This had happened before: it always

97

happened when Sam saw a rat and the rat got away. And Sam would go on barking for hours, unless he received a distraction, like a nocturnal visit from his master.

Barton rolled out of bed and staggered downstairs to the kitchen. When he switched on the light, three cats and one elderly rabbit looked up at him in surprise. Barton ignored them. He had just remembered that there was no aspirin in the house. He stepped into his Wellington boots and shrugged on his old army trench-coat over his pyjamas. Maybe the fresh air would do his head some good.

He unbolted the kitchen door and let himself out into the muddy yard beyond. Now he was outside, he could hear that Sam was scratching at the door, as well as barking. Surely the door should have been open?

Barton shook his head. He might have closed it by mistake last night, he supposed. He had been so out of his skull that he could have done anything.

He walked across the yard, calling the dog's name. The wolfhound responded by barking even more loudly; there was a series of thuds as he flung himself against the wooden door which separated him from his master.

Barton tugged at the door for several minutes, wishing he had brought a torch. He had never locked this door, all the time he had been at the farm. Still, last night was a bit exceptional in more ways than one.

After a while, he gave up. He stumbled back across the yard. He would get a torch and farm keys out of the dresser drawer. He pushed the kitchen door. It didn't move. He tried again, rattling the handle, with the same result. This was absurd: he couldn't still be *this* drunk.

Standing back, he considered what to do: smash a window, presumably, and –

He could hear something. Not the usual rustles of the night, nor even the sighing of the wind. This was some-thing else – faint, but persistent, just on the edge of sound.

The throbbing of drums?

Barton spun round. Suddenly the darkness was full of fear. He heard someone chuckle.

Then something took shape in the shadows by the gate. Something moved slowly towards him. This time, the chuckle was louder.

Sam continued to bark.

Barton began to scream.

Chapter 10

It was nine o'clock on a clear summer morning. There were no clouds in the sky – just a few wisps of black smoke.

The ambulance and the second fire engine had already left by the time Bergerac reached Barton's farm. The first fire engine remained: two firemen were hosing down the remains of the barn and of the two outhouses which adjoined it. The house itself seemed untouched.

Bergerac conferred briefly with the uniformed policeman from the local station. There was nothing new – nothing to add to the preliminary report which Bergerac had found on his desk when he got to work.

The sound of an engine on the access road leading up to the farm made him turn his head. He groaned aloud, ignoring the constable's curious glance. He would know that Rolls-Royce anywhere; every now and then, he had to resist a powerful temptation to vandalize it comprehensively.

'It's all right, Bill,' he told the constable. 'I'll deal with it.'

Hungerford got out of the car and bustled over. 'What the hell happened here, Jim?'

'Barton got himself trapped in a barn – him and his wolfhound. Apparently he had some petrol stored in there.'

Hungerford made a noise like air escaping from a tyre. 'The poor old bugger.'

Bergerac nodded. Now Hungerford was here, he might as well make himself useful. He pointed over the fields. 'Charlie – is that the only other house around here?'

'Aye.' Hungerford paused. 'You know who rents it?'

'Jersey's answer to Dennis Wheatley, I'm told. One of our more distinguished tax-exiles.'

'And he knows a lot of influential people on this island.'

'Including you, Charlie?'

Hungerford ignored the remark. He looked at his Cartier watch, automatically pushing up the cuff of his jacket so anyone with him would have to get a good look as well. 'Must rush, Jim. Committee meeting, you know.'

Bergerac himself left the farm soon after Hungerford. There was nothing more he could do here. He drove over to Bellow's place and parked on the gravel sweep by the front door. There was another Rolls-Royce parked there – older than Charlie's, but in beautiful condition.

Except for one thing.

He strolled over and examined the front nearside bumper. There was a dent in it – and probably a recent one. His mind smoothly made the connections: Bruce had been knocked down by a Rolls driven by a professional chauffeur; the chauffeur must have an employer; Bellow had a Rolls with a dent in the bumper.

It was inconclusive, of course.

A lamb bleated, somewhere out of sight.

So Barton was right about one thing. Bellow was keeping animals. Bergerac walked round the side of the house, following the sound. He passed through an archway into what had once been the farmyard. There was no one about.

He heard the bleating again. It came from the half-open door of the barn. Bergerac crossed the yard and pushed the door wide open. There were enough cages and pens in here, he thought, for a respectable Noah's Ark. And most of them were full. Bellow had a curious taste in animals.

Suddenly a deep voice spoke behind him: 'Lost, are we?'

Bergerac turned. The big man was standing on the threshold; the sunlight flattened him into a silhouette.

'I was looking for Mr Bellow.'

'You tried the front door, no doubt? I'm Bellow.'

Bergerac smiled ruefully and introduced himself. He tried the effect of a comment about the private menagerie, but got no response. Bellow intimated that it was no concern of the police. He locked the door once Bergerac was out of the barn.

'It's about the fire last night,' Bergerac explained. 'You must have had a grandstand view.'

Bellow nodded indifferently.

'But it's odd you weren't the one to call the fire brigade – being such a near neighbour.'

'I was just about to do so, Sergeant, when I heard them arriving.'

'Shame about Mr Barton.'

Bellow shrugged. 'The man was a fool.'

'You knew he'd laid a complaint against you with the police? According to him, you've been conducting experiments on animals here.'

Bellow's face was as bland as ever. 'I told you the man was a fool. So? What can I do for you? Is foul play suspected, then?' He laid an ironic stress on the words *foul play*.

Bergerac sidestepped the question. 'I simply wondered if you'd noticed anyone hanging about Barton's place. It's odd that he should have been wandering about one of his barns with his wolfhound at that time of the morning.'

'Perhaps he heard an intruder and decided to handle the matter himself, instead of phoning you people.' Bellow shrugged. 'It's just the sort of stupid thing he would have done.'

There was a note of mockery in the cultured voice. Bergerac wondered if anything could dent that massive self-confidence. Aloud he said:

'You don't mince your words, do you, Mr Bellow?'

'My words, Sergeant, are far too precious to be minced.' Bellow was not joking: he sounded as if he really meant it. 'Besides, I may be many things to many men, but a hypocrite isn't one of them. Will there be anything else?'

'Not for the moment, thanks.'

'In that case, I'm sure you can find your own way out.'

Without another word, Bellow walked slowly across to the back door. He didn't look back as he vanished into the house. Bergerac stared after him. Despite himself, he couldn't help smiling. Arrogance on that scale had its comic side, though he doubted whether Bellow was aware of it.

But Bellow was certainly an impressive man – even formidable. He had that indefinable air of always knowing something you didn't.

Bergerac's smile faded. What had Dr Frost said about Bruce? *Maybe he knew something that we don't.*

He walked back to the front of the house. A slim man with sandy hair was washing the Rolls-Royce. He was in shirt-sleeves and neatly-pressed blue trousers. He was whistling through his teeth as he worked. Bergerac's feet, crunching over the gravel, must have been clearly audible to him, but he didn't look up from his work.

'Was this the car that was involved in a fatal road accident the other day?'

The man looked up but continued polishing. 'That's right, sir.' He made the *sir* sound the next best thing to a four-letter word.

'Were you the driver then?'

The man nodded.

'So you're Gary Carter. I'm Detective Sergeant Bergerac.'

The chamois leather became still. Carter straightened

up. 'I couldn't avoid him – he ran straight out in front of me.'

'Where could he possibly have been going on that road, at that time of day? There's nothing much up there except the church.'

Carter shrugged. 'I suppose he could have been visiting old friends, sir.'

'Old friends?'

A sly smile crossed the chauffeur's face. 'There's a cemetery just over the wall from where the accident happened.'

Carter returned to his work. Bergerac gave him a hard look. *Like master, like man.*

He drove slowly back to police headquarters, his fingers drumming on the steering-wheel. If Bellow and Carter were involved, either with Bruce's death or with Barton's, their attitude simply didn't make sense. Unless, of course, they had some reason to think themselves beyond the reach of the law. Maybe Bellow was just what he seemed – a wealthy crank who could afford to indulge his whims; perhaps he got a professional kick out of obfuscation.

When he got back to headquarters, Crozier beckoned him into his office. The Chief Inspector had one of the more lurid Sunday tabloids spread open on his desk.

'Here's your answer, Jim.' Crozier tapped a heavily-illustrated feature which concerned the private lives of Arabian dancing girls. 'Jerry Bruce wasn't Bruce at all. His real name was Green. They call him Fearless Frank Green in the fleshpots of Fleet Street. He's a well-known scourge of the dissolute and guardian of public morals. In other words, he was the principal muckraker of the Sunday Yuk.'

'Then what was he doing under an assumed name here in Jersey?'

'You can ask his editor. You've just got time to meet him at the airport. Apparently Bruce was Green's usual alias when he was in the field. The editor rang up this morning – he was worried, because Green hadn't claimed any expenses for nearly a fortnight.'

Bergerac had a clear mental image of the editor of what Crozier called the Sunday Yuk. He would be obese, coarse, domineering and flashy. He would probably turn up at *Lil's Place* before the end of his stay in Jersey.

But the image was destroyed at the airport. None of the adjectives was applicable. Martin Moorhouse was a skinny middle-aged man with a scholarly stoop and a ragged moustache. His tweed jacket was nearly as old as he was. He had brown, doleful eyes which blinked a great deal.

Bergerac drove him to the mortuary, where he made the formal identification of Green's body. He had been silent in the car, but the appalling expression on the dead man's face made him want to talk. Bergerac wasn't altogether surprised: shock affected some people that way – talking to a copper could be almost as therapeutic as going to confession.

'Frank was so excited – he was on to something really big. Black magic rites with all the trimmings.'

Bergerac grinned as he opened the passenger door for Moorhouse. 'On Jersey?'

'Don't laugh, Sergeant.' Moorhouse climbed awkwardly into the car. 'An island like this is the ideal breeding ground. You've got hundreds of people here who have done everything and got everything. So they're very, very bored.' He shrugged. 'And black magic makes an ideal flavour of the month as far as they're concerned.'

Bergerac got into the driving seat and started the engine. 'I'm not convinced.'

'Frank knew his job,' Moorhouse insisted. 'Last time we spoke to him, he said the story was on the verge of breaking. Apparently he'd pulled some local girl who'd got him in on the inside. She thought he was a potential convert. A French girl.'

The car bucked forward as Bergerac let out the clutch less cautiously than usual. 'Sorry. Helene Duval?'

Moorhouse looked sharply at him. 'That's the one.'

'Did he say who else was involved?'

'As far as he could gather, there were lots of household names – in local terms, at least. And a handful of real celebrities.'

'Was one of them Bart Bellow, by any chance?'

'According to Frank, Bellow was the boss.'

It took Bergerac another half an hour to get rid of Moorhouse. The editor had no more information to give, but he scented a story; that unlikely exterior masked a highly efficient journalist. In the end, Bergerac managed to dump him on Crozier. Barney was fond of remarking that rank had its privileges; now he could deal with one of the responsibilities.

Immediately afterwards, Bergerac drove round to the bookshop. He was not surprised to find it closed. He went on to Jayston Tower.

Helene kept the door on the chain when she opened it; for a moment he thought she would refuse to let him in.

'I just want a word,' he said gently.

She unhooked the chain and held open the door. He walked through to the living-room. There were a couple of suitcases open on the sofa, both nearly full.

'Going somewhere nice?'

'Paris.' Helene picked up a shirt and began to fold it. 'My mother is sick.'

Bergerac looked at her for a moment. The bruise was less vivid today; perhaps make-up helped to disguise it. 'Tell me, how long have you known that Jerry Bruce was actually Frank Green?'

Helene turned away to lay the shirt in the suitcase. 'I don't know what you're talking about.'

'Was that the real cause of the row – when you realized he was using you to infiltrate Bart Bellow's local branch of the Magic Circle?'

She jerked upright as if he had slapped her. 'I tell you, I don't know anything about these things.' She picked up a sponge bag and crammed a handful of toilet articles into it. The toothpaste leaked on to her hand, and she swore under her breath.

'I wouldn't bother with that, Miss Duval. You aren't going anywhere.'

She started to protest, but he ignored her.

'We have every reason to believe that the death of Frank Green was no accident – and that you are a material witness. In view of that, you can forget leaving Jersey at present.'

'I am a French citizen. You have no right to hold me.'

'You want to bet?' He watched her hands; they were kneading invisible dough again. He added in a gentler voice: 'What's the matter? Scared Brother Bellow might slap a hex on you or something?'

'It isn't funny!' The colour had drained from Helene's face, accentuating the bruise.

'Oh come on. If dancing round graveyards at midnight is what turns you on, okay – that's fine. But don't tell me you actually believe this garbage?'

'You may mock. Frank mocked. At first.'

Bergerac felt his temper slipping. 'Are you trying to tell me that Green became a *real* convert? I don't believe it.'

Helene's shoulders twitched. 'Seeing is believing, Sergeant. And he saw things that made him believe.'

'A journalist like that? He was conning you, Helene.'

She shook her head. Bergerac tried to explain how the gutter press worked, but she interrupted him:

'Look, Sergeant – why do you think he was taking those pep pills?'

'Each to his own poison, I suppose.' Bergerac looked away. 'With me it was alcohol.'

'It wasn't that. He took them to stay awake. He knew what would be waiting for him if he fell asleep. Why do you think he was up by that churchyard the day he died? Bellow's place is only half a mile away. He'd been there first. He was begging Bellow to call it off. *Them*. Then he tried to reach sanctuary. But *They* got to him first.'

Bergerac tried to bring her back to earth: '*They* being the metaphysical equivalent of a cross between King Kong and the Creature from the Black Lagoon?'

'You saw what happened to him – the first time he lost consciousness.' Helene fell back in an armchair, as if she could no longer trust her legs.

'Frank Green died of heart failure,' Bergerac said patiently. 'Almost certainly, it was as a direct result of being hit by a car. The driver was Bellow's chauffeur.'

'But of course.' Helene looked pityingly at him. 'That's how it always works. That's how it worked with George Barton.'

'What do you know about the death of George Barton?'

At that moment the telephone began to ring. Helene stared at it as if the sound had mesmerized her. She made what was visibly a conscious effort and picked up the receiver.

'Hello? Hello?'

Bergerac was three yards away. He would have heard if anyone had spoken on the other end of the phone; the receiver wasn't against Helene's ear.

But there was no reply. Helene's free hand kneaded the air.

After thirty seconds, she dropped the receiver back on to its rest. 'Please, Sergeant,' she said. 'Just let me go.' There were tears in her eyes. '*Please*.'

'Certainly. Just as soon as you've given us a full and

frank statement telling us what you know about the deaths of Frank Green and George Barton.'

She stared at Bergerac without replying. There was a bleak little smile on her face with a hint of condescension in it; for an instant, it gave her face a startling resemblance to Bellow's. But Bergerac noticed her eyes. A quotation came into his mind, dredged up from God knew where in his schooldays: *Abandon hope, all ye who enter here*.

'Look, Helene,' he said more gently. 'We'll give you complete protection.'

Her eyes never left his face. 'Protection? *You*?'

She started to laugh. It sounded as if she would never be able to stop.

Chapter 11

The Triumph Roadster was in good company.

Bergerac cut the engine. On one side of him was a Bentley; on the other, a large Mercedes. Further along the gravel sweep were at least three Rolls-Royces. The red Porsche near the front door was the most common-place car he could see.

He got out of the car, closing the door quietly. It was nearly midnight, and most of the windows were dark. The exceptions were the two which belonged to the reception room to the left of the front door. Their curtains were drawn, but a crack of light seeped out where one pair failed to join. The light had an unusual quality: it was gentle and yellow. Bergerac walked over to the window and put his eye to the crack.

The first thing he noticed was the candles: there seemed to be hundreds of them. The room they illuminated was large, but it seemed smaller because of the number of people it contained.

The people belonged to the cars. Bergerac recognized a retired high court judge, the wealthiest woman in the Channel Islands and a television actor who was so famous that he had already retired three times. The crowd eddied, bringing Bellow into view: he was talking earnestly to a former General Officer Commanding Northern Ireland.

Everyone, men and women, seemed to be smoking thin, dark cigars. Most of them were drinking as well. Bergerac craned his head and saw Carter standing behind a table parallel with the wall. The chauffeur was ladling what looked like an orange-based punch into the glass of a pearl-encrusted dowager. A small rostrum had been set

110

up to the right of Carter's table. It was empty, except for three African drums.

Bergerac moved from the window to the front door. It took nearly a minute for Carter to answer his ring. The chauffeur was obviously reluctant to let Bergerac come in, but lacked the assurance to turn him away. Bergerac pushed past him into the hall. A buzz of conversation came through the half-open door to the reception room. There was a sweet, heavy smell in the air.

Carter made the best of a bad job and ushered Bergerac into Bellow's study, which was opposite the room where the party was. It was a sombre room, furnished conservatively and expensively. There was a copy of *Demonkind* on a side table. Bergerac thumbed through it while he waited for his host.

'Yes, Sergeant?' came a deep voice from the doorway.

Bellow in his dinner jacket was an impressive figure. Bergerac tossed the book back on the table and said pleasantly:

'I've come about Jerry Bruce – or should I say Frank Green?'

Bellow's face betrayed not the slightest reaction. Bergerac went on:

'The one your chauffeur ran down. Did you realize that he was an investigative journalist? And that you were the one he was investigating?'

Bellow shrugged. 'The endless attentions of the gutter press are part of the price of fame.'

'It's a price worth paying, I imagine,' Bergerac said blandly. He tapped the cover of *Demonkind*. 'Bearing in mind the sort of money you must get for writing this guff.'

It was a crude attempt to get a rise out of Bellow, but Bergerac reckoned he could safely rely on his host's monumental egotism. He was not disappointed.

'Guff, Sergeant?' There was a hint of amusement in

the rich voice – and more than a hint of patronage. 'Is that how you see it?'

Bergerac grinned. 'Raising the devil?' he said scornfully. 'Spells and incantations? We're living in the twentieth century, you know.'

'Is the idea of casting a spell very different from the standard Christian practice of praying to a plaster saint?'

'I wouldn't know.' Bergerac's smile broadened. 'I've never felt the urge to try that, either.'

'You must come round some time, Sergeant – let us try to convert you.'

Bergerac's face was suddenly hard. 'Like you did with Frank Green?'

'I'm sorry, Sergeant, I'm afraid I don't know what you mean.' The silence between them lengthened and became oppressive. 'And now, if there's nothing else, I really should be getting back to my guests.'

On this occasion, Bellow didn't tell Bergerac to find his own way out. He accompanied him to the front door. The clean night air contrasted sharply with the smoky atmosphere in the house.

On the threshold, Bergerac turned back, almost bumping into Bellow. He nodded towards the reception room. 'Monthly meeting of the local coven?'

Bellow's impassivity showed signs of cracking. Like most people who took themselves too seriously, he was vulnerable to ridicule.

Bergerac waved a hand towards the parked cars. 'I must say you've come a long way since broomsticks.'

'You would be wise not to be facetious, Sergeant,' Bellow spat, 'about things of which you know nothing.'

'Or else you'll send something unspeakable from the Outer Circle round to see me?' Bergerac paused and looked directly at his host. When he spoke again it was deliberately, with no trace of flippancy: '*Next time I nod off?*'

112

Bellow began to close the door. 'Goodnight, Sergeant.' Just before the door closed, he said something else, which Bergerac had to strain to catch: 'Sweet dreams.'

Bergerac got into his car. The night was warm, and the hood was down. Just before he started the engine, he heard something.

The deep, rhythmic murmur of drums.

Crozier didn't like it at all.

The habitual frown deepened on his forehead as Bergerac talked. When Peggy came into the office, Crozier snapped at her for being two minutes late and sent her to get them some coffee.

He turned back to Bergerac. 'You think they killed Green *and* Barton?' he demanded incredulously.

'They killed Green because he was about to blow the gaff on what goes on at Bart Bellow's nasty little cocktail parties. I don't know what does go on besides mumbo jumbo, but animal sacrifice and drug-taking both look probable. As for Barton, they killed him because he was harassing them – and, even worse, he was drawing attention to them.'

'He must be mad,' Crozier said pettishly. 'Or you are.'

'He's the one who's mad – have you read his latest book? Bellow's as serious as they make them, believe me.'

Peggy came in with the coffee. Bergerac thanked her with a smile, but Crozier didn't even look up.

Bergerac glanced at the clock on the wall: it was nearly nine already. He wanted to get moving, but he needed Crozier's approval first. He tried another angle:

'There's another consideration, you know. Judging by the cars I saw last night, and the guests I recognized, some very wealthy people will have a lot to lose if this business ever hits the front pages.'

113

Crozier sighed, tacitly conceding the force of the argument. 'What makes you think they'll have a go at Helene Duval next?'

'After what I told Bellow last night, he'll feel there's no alternative – I let slip some information which Bellow knows she must have given me.'

'Not exactly ethical.'

'Neither are two murders.'

'Just make sure it isn't three.'

'No sweat.' Privately, Bergerac was considerably relieved: it would have been awkward if Crozier had decided not to back him. Worse, it might have been fatal for Helene Duval. Aloud he said: 'I've had Duval's flat under surveillance since last night.'

Crozier raised his eyebrows but said nothing: a decision involving a two-man, twenty-four-hour surveillance was not normally made at Detective Sergeant level. All he said was: 'I hope they're suitably equipped with crucifixes and cloves of garlic.'

Bergerac grinned. 'So it's beginning to get to you as well?'

'Who's at Jayston Tower at present?'

'Wilson and Nick Paris – that new boy the Met sent us. I'm taking over with Goddard at nine-thirty.'

Crozier looked up at the clock. 'What's keeping you? You'll be late.'

A few minutes later, Bergerac and Goddard left headquarters in the former's car. Bergerac parked in a side road a quarter of a mile away from the flats; there was no point in advertising their presence. Goddard said little as they walked the rest of the way to Jayston Tower. He was a stolid, reliable man with whom Bergerac had worked increasingly closely during the last few months.

The unmarked police car was parked on the opposite side of the road from the flats' entrance. Wilson had chosen the position well, Bergerac thought: from the car you could see both the foyer and the small side door which the caretaker used.

Before getting into the back of the car, Bergerac glanced up at the fourth floor. Two of the windows there belonged to Helene's flat – probably to the kitchen and bathroom, since the main rooms faced the sea. Both sets of curtains were still drawn.

Wilson turned round as Bergerac slid into the car. 'Nothing to report, Jim. The couple from Two A got back in the earlier hours – could have pulled 'em in for drunken driving. Since then we've had the milkman and the postman going in and coming out, and a general exodus of workers between eight-thirty and nine. No sign of our lady.'

'Okay, Terry. Off you go.'

Wilson and Paris got out. Bergerac and Goddard took their places, with Goddard behind the steering-wheel. The hours passed slowly, with each man doing a half-hour spell of observation while the other read or dozed. The interior of the car grew heavy with the stale smoke from Goddard's cigarettes, despite the fact that they kept the windows open. There was little wind and, as the sun climbed higher, Bergerac thought longingly of the beach.

The car heated up. The plastic of the seats felt sticky to their touch. Both men were down to their shirt-sleeves. Bergerac flicked through yesterday's Jersey *Evening Post* for the second time. He tossed the paper on to the back seat and picked up the *Guardian*. He noticed with distaste that his fingers were grey with newsprint. He turned to the crossword and methodically worked his way through the clues. It didn't take long because the only one he could do was 23 Across.

Goddard touched his arm.

Bergerac let the newspaper drop to his lap. A woman was walking along the pavement. She wore some sort of uniform – a dusky pink affair, topped with a cherry-red beret. From her hand swung a small briefcase with a logo on the side. As they watched she began to climb the shallow flight of steps which led up to the main entrance of Jayston Tower.

Bergerac glanced at Goddard, with a puzzled expression on his face. The logo looked familiar, but he couldn't for the life of him place it.

'It's one of those telephone cleaning companies,' Goddard muttered, his eyes never leaving the door. 'They do my wife's office. Presumably when you're rich and lazy, they do home phones as well.'

'Looks innocent enough. Let's not do anything hasty.' This was always a problem with surveillance work, he thought – you had to walk a tightrope between the complementary dangers of over-reacting and under-reacting.

The woman went into the foyer. The heavy doors swung back behind her, cutting off the view of the two policemen.

The seconds ticked away, turning into minutes. Bergerac did not return to the crossword. He was uncomfortably conscious of a trickle of sweat working its way down between his shoulder blades.

A Ford with Jersey number-plates came up behind them. It pulled over and parked immediately outside the main entrance. At precisely the same moment, the doors opened and Helene Duval came out.

She hurried down the steps, her long black hair swinging across her face. She was wearing a bright summer dress but was carrying nothing – not even a handbag. The Ford's passenger door swung open; the neat timing suggested premeditation.

'That's her, Barry. And the bloke with her is Carter.'

Goddard had already started the engine. 'Whatever she's doing, she's doing it willingly.'

The Ford pulled away from the pavement, its tyres screeching on the warm soft tarmac.

'Don't lose them, Barry,' Bergerac snapped.

The police car surged after the Ford, keeping well back. With luck, St Helier's midday traffic would give them the cover they needed.

Bergerac tried to relax. He knew Goddard was one of the best pursuit drivers at the Bureau. But what the hell was Helene doing? Yesterday she had been terrified of Bellow and – by extension – of Carter; after all, in her eyes, both men served the same supernatural master.

Then why was she running away with Carter, of her own free will?

Chapter 12

The old debate was going round and round Helene Duval's mind with the monotonous regularity of a hamster on its wheel.

The question was whether waiting for *Them* to come was worse than what would happen when *They* arrived. Sometimes she thought that nothing could possibly be worse than this waiting. On the other hand, she knew from experience that *They* had a nasty habit of exceeding your expectations.

Jerry would know the answer. Though he wasn't Jerry, of course, but Frank. Or even George Barton. But neither of them was available. She began to cry again – this time not just for herself, but for the hopes she had lost when Jerry turned out to be someone else.

She had eaten nothing for nearly twenty hours. The dull, tense ache in her stomach was at least partly due to the pints of strong black coffee she had poured into it since Sergeant Bergerac left her. If only she had some of the speed Jerry had used – though that hadn't saved him in the end.

Nothing could save you when *They* were angry.

Two-thirds of the gin bottle was empty now. As a rule, she hated gin – she only had it in the flat for visitors. As she poured, the bottle chinked against the rim of the glass, producing a high, clear note which reminded her of the bell they rang at the elevation of the host when she was a child. The memory – of the little church in Avranches, of herself in a white dress, of her parents, towering on either side of her childhood self, protective in their Sunday best – started her crying again.

The glass clattered against her teeth as she drank. She had no fear of drinking herself into vulnerable oblivion – the alcohol seemed to have no effect on her. Certainly it failed as an anaesthetic.

Usually the empty bottles and dirty mugs which littered the sitting-room would have made her uncomfortable until she had cleared them away. But now she couldn't care less. Her gaze kept returning to the two half-packed suitcases which mocked her on the sofa. She had been naïve to think she could ever escape. There was nowhere she could find safety; there was no one who could protect her.

Once or twice she had thought of using the telephone. She had even got as far as beginning to dial. But Bellow was as implacable as the powers he served. And Bergerac in his unbelief was worse than useless. One wouldn't help her, and the other couldn't.

At that moment, the telephone began to ring.

The glass slipped from Helene's hand and fell with a thud on the carpet. The thick pile cushioned the fall. The glass did not break, but rolled a few inches, spreading a dark stain of gin over the delicate Chinese pattern.

The ringing went on, filling her head with a harsh jangling – a discordant carillon for the church of Satan. The sounds reverberated, seeming to grow ever louder as they bounced back on one another. When the clangour grew beyond a certain point, she knew intuitively, she would become mad. And if she was mad, her final defence against *Them* would have crumbled.

She picked up the phone.

There was a moment of blessed silence. Somewhere outside the flat a seagull cried. Then all relief was abruptly destroyed.

'Helene? *They* are coming for you now, Helene.' Bellow's rich voice held a caressing note. As always, she

119

found it hypnotic. 'Helene . . . *They* can't wait for you to go to sleep. *They* are coming for you, now, Helene . . .'

Silence returned. Helene looked stupidly at the receiver, now back on its rest. Had she put the phone down first, or had Bellow? The answer didn't matter, but the question kept the terror at bay for an instant.

But only for an instant.

Someone in the room was making a high keening noise. Helene looked wildly around. It could only be herself – there was no one else: unless *They* were already here.

The possibility forced her to act. She struggled out of the chair and stumbled towards the door, tripping over the glass on her way. Once in the hall, she clawed at the lock, the bolts and the chain which guarded the front door from all earthly visitors. The cold metal had become alive and malign: her fingers fumbled for what seemed like hours.

One bolt scraped back. The other followed. The chain took longer, but she managed it at last. The final hurdle was the lock. It remained jammed. Helene gave up and hammered futilely against the door.

The pain brought back a fragment of memory: last night she had double-locked the door. She ran back to the sitting-room for her handbag. The key was resting on top of her passport. Her hands were shaking so much that she could hardly pick it up. With an immense effort of will, she managed to coordinate her fingers. She carried the key carefully into the hall, and unlocked the door.

The lift was waiting for her.

She ran into it and hammered at the button for the ground floor. With a hiss, the doors closed. Helene fell back against the wall, her head lolling to one side. The lift moved slowly downwards.

Five seconds later, it stopped. The doors remained closed. Once again, someone was keening.

Helene flung herself at the controls and punched the ground-floor button repeatedly. Nothing happened.

'Please,' she whimpered. 'Please don't hurt me. Please.'

She banged against the doors of the lift with the palms of her hands. It had no effect, except that the metal surface seemed to be growing warmer by the second. She leant against the doors, the fight seeping out of her. She was in her coffin, she realized, a vertical coffin framed with steel.

It was then that she noticed the small panel set in the side of the lift above the control buttons. It was labelled *Emergency Telephone*.

She swore at her own stupidity and tore open the panel. There was a red telephone inside. She seized it with a sob of relief. The handset came away from its base. She felt something brush against the uncovered skin of her forearm. She looked down.

From the handset dangled eighteen inches of wire. At the other end was nothing. The cord had been cut.

It was growing hotter in the lift. It seemed harder to breathe. Her eyes watered, and she could smell smoke. *They* had lit her funeral pyre.

'No, oh please no,' she pleaded, talking into the handset which connected her with nothing. 'I'm sorry, please don't hurt me, I didn't mean it.'

Then, apart from the crackling of the fire far below, there was silence.

For the first quarter of an hour, the Ford drove aimlessly through St Helier, backtracking several times. Bergerac was worried. It was behaviour designed to show up a tail.

Carter turned down towards the harbour but, at the bus station, he turned left and plunged into the tunnel beneath Fort Regent. He carried on along La Route du Fort. At the five-road junction he took the A3.

As the Ford headed west out of St Helier it picked up speed.

'Where the hell's he going?' Goddard said. 'Grouville? Gorey?'

'For all I know, they're going to gawp at the tableaux at Mont Orgueil Castle.' Bergerac spoke absently, his eyes on the car ahead. 'You know, Barry, there's something not kosher about all this. If – '

'Damn,' Goddard interrupted. 'I think he's spotted me.'

Up to now, the Ford had kept well within the speed limits. Now it was rapidly drawing away from the police car.

'Okay, pull him over.' Bergerac was glad of the excuse: a suspicion was growing in his mind.

Goddard flashed his lights and tried a quick burst of the siren. Carter responded by putting his foot down even more on the accelerator.

'Well, well,' Goddard said. 'He doesn't seem to like that idea.'

'Persuade him,' Bergerac suggested.

The two cars roared west down the A3. Fortunately there was relatively little traffic at that time of day. The standard 2-litre engine of the Ford didn't stand a chance against the customized job under the bonnet of the surveillance car. Three minutes later, Goddard overtook the Ford, narrowly missing an eastbound articulated lorry in the process.

Carter recognized defeat and pulled over. The police car stopped ten yards ahead. Bergerac and Goddard leapt out and ran back to the Ford, one on each side. Bergerac pulled open the driver's door.

'What's your game?' Carter demanded. He was a model of injured innocence. Then his eyes widened as he pretended to recognize Bergerac. 'Oh, it's *you*, Sergeant. Just a minute.' He turned to the woman beside him. 'It's

Sergeant Bergerac, love.' He gave her an avuncular pat on the knee and got out of the car. 'I didn't realize you were the police, or I'd have stopped sooner.'

For a moment, Bergerac didn't reply. He was looking at the woman. Her face bore no real resemblance to Helene's. The long black hair was probably a wig. Her figure was similar to Helene's, and the dress looked like her taste. Bellow had been clever: no one really looks closely at a person in uniform – you don't see beyond the clothes, as a rule. The wig and the dress would have been in the suitcase. The woman must have done a quick change in the foyer – perhaps using the telephone booth near the stairs.

It was the perfect decoy – *leaving Helene alone and unguarded*.

'You're nicked,' he told Carter curtly. 'Both of you. Barry, take 'em back to the office and hold 'em.'

He sprinted back to the police car. As he ran, Carter called after him: 'On what charge?'

Goddard smiled comfortably. 'I'll think of something. Don't you worry your head about it. Will you drive or shall I?'

The door of the police car slammed. Bergerac switched on the headlights and siren and did a U-turn into the eastbound traffic. On the open road he held the car steady at ninety m.p.h. As he drove he used the shortwave to call headquarters. Crozier promised to send a squad car right away. Bergerac swiftly calculated the logistics involved. Unless a car was already in the area, it was unlikely that reinforcements would get to Jayston Tower before he himself did.

Every second could count: every second could be shortening Helene's life.

He drew up outside the flats with a screech of burning rubber. Leaving the engine running and the door open, he pounded up the steps into the foyer. Behind him, the siren drowned the calls of the gulls.

Thick black smoke rushed out to meet him as soon as he opened the door. He ran across to the lift. The shaft doors were closed. The indicator light for the third floor was on. A red light pulsed above the door. Somewhere in the basement, an alarm bell was ringing.

'Bellow! Where are you? The game's over!'

There was no reply to his shout. Bergerac took the stairs, three at a time. On the first floor, the smoke was worse. On the second landing it was so thick that he could hardly see.

Bergerac, coughing violently, forced his way to the lift shaft. The doors had been propped open with a chair. Through the gap poured a choking stream of oily smoke. He wrenched back both doors. Far below, he could see flames flickering at the base of the shaft. Ignoring his watering eyes, he looked upwards. The cables snaked up to the lift itself. It was jammed between this floor and the one above.

And Helene?

Bergerac pulled back from the shaft just as Bellow plunged out of the smoke, his arms outstretched. His face was blackened; his lips were open in a sneer which revealed his startlingly white teeth; the eyes seemed to blaze in reflection of the fire below.

The huge hands with their long, powerful fingers were aiming for Bergerac's throat. Two seconds earlier, and a simple push in the small of the back would have been enough. Bergerac, already turning, swerved to the left. Only one of Bellow's hands made contact. Bergerac seized the wrist with both hands and twisted with all his force.

The manoeuvre rotated the two struggling men through a hundred and eighty degrees. Bellow, his back to the open lift shaft, kicked up at Bergerac's crotch. Bergerac advanced to meet the kick, catching it harmlessly on his thigh. Automatically, he made a counter-attack, chopping across at Bellow's throat.

Bellow was already off-balance because of the abortive kick. He saw the blow coming, and tried to back away. The side of Bergerac's hand caught him just above the Adam's apple.

The big man toppled backwards in slow motion. For an instant, he looked stupefied, as if he simply couldn't believe that *They* were allowing this to happen to him. He fell with his arms outstretched into a black featherbed of smoke. Suddenly his face contorted with fear and a scream – shockingly high for a man with such a deep-pitched voice – rose up the lift shaft as its source fell down it.

Far below there was a crash and a blinding spurt of flame. Tongues of fire licked up the shaft for a second. Then there was complete darkness.

The chair had gone down the shaft with Bellow. The shaft doors hissed shut. The smoke seemed to be clearing with astonishing speed. Bergerac's hand was shaking as he pressed the lift's call button.

The lift juddered to a halt on the second floor. The doors opened. Bergerac stumbled in. Helene lay against the wall furthest from the doors, huddled in the foetal position. The air in the lift tasted strangely sweet, though the smoke had left black smears on the walls and ceiling.

He pulled Helene on to the landing. Her face was drained of blood, but she was still breathing – regularly and deeply, as if asleep. Bergerac frowned: that was curious, for her lungs must have been starved of oxygen. The palms of both her hands were bloodied; obviously her panic had driven her to dig her long nails into them.

Bergerac patted her cheeks and, in under a minute, she came round. Outside another siren was wailing: reinforcements had arrived.

Her large, blue eyes stared up at Bergerac. They were guileless and untroubled. Suddenly she smiled. 'Sergeant Bergerac,' she said softly. 'So you could protect me, after all.'

Bergerac looked up at the clock and grinned to himself. It was half-past five. Against all expectations, it looked as if he would be able to keep to the arrangements he had made with Susan last weekend. They planned to try a new seafood restaurant in St Brelade. Jean-Luc, Lil's headwaiter, raved about it, which meant it had to be good. Usually he was scornful about any other cooking than his own.

There was a rustle of paper as Crozier, on the other side of the desk, turned to the last page of Bergerac's interim report on the Bellow case. A few seconds later, he pulled out a biro and initialled each page.

He looked up at Bergerac. 'Thank God we didn't have to bring this nutter to trial. He must have been insane, despite his clever little tricks. How did he think he'd get away with it?'

'We couldn't have pinned a thing on him for the first two murders,' Bergerac pointed out. 'Suspicion isn't proof. And he very nearly got away with the third.'

'He took a lot of unnecessary risks, doing it in a place like that.'

'Not really. Jayston Tower is practically empty during the weekdays – most of the residents are young upwardly-mobile professionals with jobs to go to. Bellow used bribes and browbeating to get the caretaker in his pocket. Both Carter and the woman they used as a decoy are loyal disciples. If Bellow hadn't died, they wouldn't have talked.'

'What did he use to start the fire?'

'Carter says oil, petrol and a couple of old mattresses.'

Bergerac paused. 'He also says Bellow invoked supernatural help for it. You know – called in the Satanic flamethrowers. You have to admit, there was an awful lot of smoke for such a relatively small fire.'

Crozier snorted contemptuously. 'Rubbish. These things are all a matter of draught and fuel and so on. Perfectly normal.'

'I suppose so.' Bergerac hesitated. 'But – '

Crozier threw up his hands. 'Don't tell me you're becoming a last-minute convert to the faith.'

Bergerac shrugged. 'It was odd the way the fire went out, just when Bellow was killed.'

'I checked with the Fire Brigade. It can happen. A sudden flash uses up all the available oxygen and snuffs out the fire.'

'There's always a rational explanation for these things.' Bergerac glanced at the clock and decided not to mention how quickly the smoke had cleared or the speed of Helene's recovery. No doubt there were rational explanations about these things as well.

Crozier nodded. 'Of course.'

Bergerac got up, yanking his jacket from the back of the chair. In the doorway he paused, his mind still on Bellow's death. He turned back to Crozier, his lips twitching.

'But it was a hell of a way to go.'

Chapter 13

Bergerac stared obliquely through the car windscreen at the open-air café on the other side of the road. It was August, and all but a few of the tables were occupied. Tourists were the main clientele. Since the Havre des Pas beach was less than a hundred yards away, many of them were in varying stages of undress. Bergerac tried to calculate the time they had been on the island by the pinkness of their skins.

In the passenger seat beside him, Crozier clicked his tongue against the roof of his mouth. The Chief Inspector, never a patient man, was becoming tetchy.

A waitress worked her way among the crowded tables, piling dirty crockery on to a tray. As Bergerac watched her, she paused at Van Rijn's table.

Van Rijn – a hard-fleshed, stocky man with a short beard and a weather-beaten complexion – was clearly nearly as impatient as Crozier was. For the last half-hour, the Dutchman had been drinking cups of coffee he didn't want, glancing at his watch and chain-smoking.

The waitress moved away. Bergerac glanced along the row of tables. Goddard and Paris were at the front of the café, strategically placed by the entrance. Both were in plainclothes – but both looked overdressed in this setting.

Crozier stirred beside him. 'Twenty-three minutes late.' He made it sound like an accusation – levelled at Bergerac. 'I think your friend was having you on.'

Bergerac's hands tightened on the steering-wheel. 'Look,' he said soothingly. 'He got the right place and the right man.'

'And the wrong time? Face it, Jim, if your little friend

is right about what Van Rijn is carrying, the lady's not going to take time out to have her hair done before she turns up.'

Both men looked across the road. Van Rijn had put the packet on the table. From here, the wrapping looked like sheets of newspaper.

'Okay, *Chief* Inspector. If you've got some brilliant idea about what our next move should be, I'm always willing to hear it.'

Bergerac could feel his temper slipping away from his control. He had had no sleep for thirty hours. He and Susan had planned a quiet night at home last night, but an AA phone call had changed all that. Bergerac had spent the hours of darkness being a combination of nurse, friend and gaoler to a local vicar whose craving for distilled spirits had broken out again. When he got home after dawn, he and Susan had had their first real argument; somehow he hadn't felt like sleeping after that. And now this job was turning sour on them – and Crozier had already elected him as the potential scapegoat.

The Chief Inspector dabbed at his forehead with a handkerchief. 'I suppose there's not much we can do – except wait and see if he makes any kind of move.'

Bergerac thwacked the steering-wheel with the palm of his hand. 'Now why didn't *I* think of that.'

The sarcasm didn't improve the atmosphere between the two men. Five more minutes passed. It was obvious that Van Rijn was becoming increasingly nervous. When the waitress arrived with another cup of coffee for him, he stood up abruptly. Ignoring the coffee, he thrust a note into her hand, picked up the package, and walked swiftly towards the exit.

Bergerac and Crozier stiffened. To Bergerac's amazement, Paris leapt to his feet as Van Rijn passed his table. The policeman's thin cockney voice carried easily through the car's open window.

'Hey, you! Just a minute.' Paris shrugged off Goddard's restraining arm and took half a step forward.

Bergerac started the engine.

In the same instant, Van Rijn turned, his left hand balling into a fist. He drove it into Paris's stomach and ran frantically into the street.

Bergerac rammed the stick into first gear, let out the clutch and cut across the sailor's path. Unable to stop, Van Rijn crashed against the car and sprawled over the bonnet. The package flew out of his hand. Before it hit the ground, Bergerac was out of the car.

The package thudded on to the tarmac. Bergerac picked it up. 'Wouldn't want anything to happen to these, would we?'

Van Rijn stared at him with fear in his eyes. Crozier was already behind him, holding him down with an armlock. Goddard ran across the road. Paris walked behind, clutching his stomach.

'Cuff him,' Crozier told Goddard. 'Then you two clowns can take him back to headquarters. Come on, Jim.'

Goddard, Paris and Van Rijn walked back to the second car, ignoring the excited questions of the small crowd which had already gathered. Crozier and Bergerac drove to headquarters with the package. If they were right about the contents, it was not the sort of thing to take chances with.

They took it into Crozier's office. Bergerac put it on the desk and cut the string. He tore his way through several sheets of an Amsterdam daily newspaper. At last there was a layer of cotton wool. He lifted it gently away. Underneath, two engraving-plates nestled side by side on another layer of cotton wool. One by one, he held them up to the light, inspecting them for damage.

Behind the desk, Crozier gave a dry chuckle. 'I think the Dutch treasury might have forgiven us if we'd dented them. They were supposed to be destroyed six months ago.'

Bergerac grinned. The partial success of the operation had improved his temper. 'Tempting, isn't it?' he said dreamily. 'I've always fancied retiring abroad and printing my own money.'

'Ye-es,' Crozier said slowly, as if he was giving the idea serious thought. 'I can just see you – tiptoeing through the tulips and gazing at windmills – ' A knock on the door interrupted this unusual attempt at humour. He called: 'Come!'

Peggy stuck her head round the door. 'It's Constable Paris, sir. He'd like a word with you.'

'Would he?' There was a gleam in Crozier's eye. 'Good – I'd like a word with him.'

Paris sidled through the door and pulled himself to attention in front of the desk. He was a tall thin man with sallow skin and closely-cropped grey hair.

'Well, Constable Paris?'

'I just wanted to say I was sorry, sir – for jumping the gun like that.'

'I should bloody well think you were. What were you doing?'

Paris shifted uneasily. 'Well, sir . . . I was afraid we might lose him – him and the plates. I just thought – '

Crozier interrupted him with a distinctly theatrical sigh. 'Look, Paris: I know you're a new boy round here, but I would have thought there was one significant difference between Jersey and the Met that wouldn't need spelling out to anybody.' He saw that Paris was looking blankly at him and nodded to Bergerac. 'Tell him, Jim.'

'It's an island, Nick,' Bergerac explained. 'People can't just slip down a tube station and disappear. They have to get on a boat or a plane – which gives us a ninety-five per cent chance of picking them up.'

'And on this occasion,' Crozier said harshly, 'we might

131

have managed to slip a discreet tail on him. It's just possible that Van Rijn might have led us to the Costain woman. As it is, we'll never tie her in with it, not in a hundred years.'

'Has Van Rijn said anything?' Paris asked hopefully.

At a nod from Crozier, Bergerac took over again. Van Rijn, he told Paris, was just a delivery boy. He didn't even know what he was carrying, let alone whom it was for. He had given them a description of his Amsterdam contact, but that was hardly going to help the Jersey police.

Paris looked rueful. 'Look, I really am sorry. If there's anything I can do . . .' His voice trailed away, rising slightly.

'Well,' said Crozier, with massive sarcasm, 'that's really *nice* of you, Constable Paris. But unless you can come up with a foolproof method of planting something other than a parking ticket on the oh-so-respectable Mrs Costain, I don't think there's a lot you can do for us, just at the moment.'

'Well, that's a bit of a tall order, sir,' Paris said seriously. He seemed not to notice that his superiors were looking with fascination at him. 'She was operating in the Smoke all the time I was on the Met. We were never able to pin *anything* on her.'

Bergerac tried not to look at Crozier as this magnificent example of Metropolitan morality was displayed for his edification. There was a moment of silence. Finally, Crozier said:

'That's it, then. Obviously we might as well forget the whole thing. Just remember, this isn't the Met.' Paris tried to say something, and Crozier's restraint deserted him. His voice rose to a roar: 'Go on – get out!'

Paris scuttled out of the office. Crozier sank back in his chair. As soon as the door had closed, he said: 'If anyone ever talks to me about cockney shrewdness again, I'll

throttle him. I've seldom seen a more convincing argument for local recruitment.'

'He's all right.' Bergerac could remember what the first
few weeks on a new job felt like. And Paris hadn't exactly
got a lot of social graces. 'I expect he was just trying to
make an impression.'

Crozier shrugged, dismissing the subject of Paris and
returning to the plates. 'So – what do you think went
wrong? If it was a tip-off, we have to look at Leech. He's
your snout.'

'You think he could be playing both ends against the
middle?'

'Yeah. He gives us the plates to keep us sweet, and
then warns Costain not to show up and collect them.'

'Possible.' Bergerac got to his feet. 'Leech and that
little blonde of his were due to leave the island this
afternoon. Maybe I'll go and help them pack.'

'You do that,' said Crozier heavily. He scooped up the
plates and laid them back on their cotton wool bed. 'In
the meantime, I'll lock these up where they won't be a
temptation to anybody.'

Omdurman Road was tucked away near the gas works.
By St Helier's admittedly high standards, it was on the
wrong side of shabby.

Bergerac pulled the Triumph over to the kerb. Sam
Leech had a flat in what had once been a single house.
The conversion job had been done too cheaply and too
long ago. Goddard offered to come in with him, but
Bergerac shook his head.

'You cover the back, Barry. Just in case he's feeling
coy.'

The front door was common to all the flats and was
always left open. Leech had a flat on the ground floor, at
the back. There were several layers of paint on the flat's

133

front door, revealed like archaeological layers by uneven peeling.

Bergerac didn't bother to knock: this wasn't a social call. He barged through the door, shouting for Sam.

But the room beyond was empty of people. It was in its usual state of squalor. The remains of at least three meals were on the table by the window; gorged flies patrolled the airspace above the plates. Records out of their sleeves were strewn over the stained carpet. There were two rucksacks on the hearthrug, surrounded by piles of unfolded clothes.

'Sam?' Bergerac called again. 'Midge?'

Again, there was no reply. He moved into the centre of the room, and suddenly froze. Somewhere in the flat, a woman was talking, in a low, urgent voice. He called out, but there was no response.

He tracked the voice through a door in the opposite wall to a small lobby. Two open doors gave on to a kitchen and a bedroom; the third door was shut. He opened it.

Midge Harris was sitting on the floor, squeezed between the lavatory pan and the wall. She had drawn her knees up to her chin and clasped them tightly with her arms.

'Midge?'

She looked up at him. She was in her early twenties, and had a conventionally – if vacuously – pretty face.

'It's all right,' she said in a monotone, as if repeating a lesson. 'We're going to Cornwall to stay with my brother. He's got a job fixed up for Sam and everything. No problem.'

'It's okay, Midge.' Bergerac moved slowly towards her.

Her vacant eyes slid sideways. 'Trouble is, the lazy sod won't get out of the bath. You tell him, Sergeant – tell him to get out.'

Bergerac followed the direction of her gaze. The bath was behind the door. Over its white enamel side dangled what had once been a human arm. Along the side of the bath, a thin red puddle showed starkly against the green linoleum.

It was worse in the bath itself – much worse.

There were more flies in here than there were in the living-room.

'Dear God,' Bergerac said quietly. He raised the window and shouted for Barry.

Midge's head swung slowly from side to side, as if she was trying to shake something out of it. 'Sam?' she said plaintively. 'Hurry up – we're going to miss the plane.'

Goddard had never seen Bergerac so angry.

As the hours passed, his rage seemed to increase. Once the scene-of-the-crime team and the ambulance were there, the two plainclothesmen were supposed to return to headquarters to report.

But Bergerac drove across town in the opposite direction, to a leafy residential street where the villas stood well back in their own grounds. Goddard knew the address Bergerac was making for: he had seen the file. Bergerac pulled up in the drive with a jerk that sent the gravel spurting beneath the Triumph's tyres.

Goddard grabbed his arm. 'For God's sake, Jim – there's nothing you can do. There's no proof.'

'Get off my back, Barry.' Bergerac pushed Goddard aside, got out of the car and leant against the front-door bell.

An elderly manservant opened the door. 'Good afternoon, sir.' He sounded like a Hollywood extra.

'Where's Mrs Costain?'

'I'm afraid Mrs Costain is not – '

Bergerac pushed past the servant into the hall. The old man tried to protest, but Bergerac ignored him. At the far end of the hall, a pair of sliding glass doors stood open, framing the blue waters of a swimming-pool.

Bergerac marched through the doors with Goddard close behind him. The manservant followed, his face working. There were two people by the pool: a tall bony woman with dark hair and an angular face; and a large, thickset man who was chewing the side of his thumb. The woman was wearing a black, one-piece bathing suit and had her feet up on a reclining chair. Her companion wore a dark, ill-fitting suit and looked like an undertaker fallen on evil days.

The woman looked up. 'What the hell's going on?'

'Are you Mary Lou Costain?' Bergerac demanded.

'Mrs Costain, yes. Who the hell are you?'

Bergerac paused. Behind him, the servant twittered apologetically. Now he was here, he had to try to keep it official. 'My name is Bergerac. I'm a Sergeant with the Jersey police.'

'Really.' Mrs Costain set down her glass on the cast-iron table beside her chair. 'And that gives you the right to come barging in here like a mad bull?' Her cold, slanting eyes moved across to the servant. 'All right, Thomas,' she said wearily. 'Just go away.' As the servant shuffled into the house, Mrs Costain turned back to Bergerac. 'Congratulations, Sergeant. You've just cost that silly old man his job.'

'That doesn't surprise me, Mrs Costain.' Bergerac took a step forward. 'Getting rid of people who annoy you is one of your specialities. Take Sam Leech, for instance. He worked for you, didn't he?'

Mrs Costain shrugged. She took another sip from her drink before replying. 'There was a man named Leech who used to run errands for me. I didn't think he was altogether – how shall I put it? – trustworthy. So I fired him. Is he in some sort of trouble?'

'He's dead.'

'Really?' Mrs Costain raised her perfectly-plucked eyebrows. 'Is there something else you want me to say?'

136

'It really doesn't bother you?'

Mrs Costain lay back in her chair and reached for the sun-tan lotion. 'Why should it? I'm sorry if you think I'm callous.'

'Callous isn't the word for you.' Bergerac controlled his voice with an effort. 'Let's stop pussyfooting, Mrs Costain. You and I both know that three months ago a disgruntled employee of the Dutch mint walked off with some currency plates that were due to go to the grinder. He put them up for sale to the highest bidder. And that bidder turned out to be you.'

Mrs Costain massaged oil into her forearm. She gave no sign that she was listening.

'Sam Leech has worked for me in the past,' Bergerac continued. 'Yesterday he rang me up to say you were expecting a delivery. We turned up – and so did the man with the plates. But there was no sign of you, or any of your people.'

'That's hardly surprising.' Mrs Costain capped the bottle. 'It's the first I've heard of this extraordinary story.'

'I went to see Sam, to ask him what happened. But he couldn't tell me anything, because he was dead. Do you find that extraordinary too, Mrs Costain?'

'Perhaps he committed suicide out of remorse for telling all those lies about me.'

'You think so?' By now, Bergerac's face was white with anger. 'You think he slashed himself with a razor blade in twenty different places and then just lay there, bleeding to death?'

Goddard was watching the bodyguard. His name was Liddell; in the flesh he was even uglier than his photograph in the file suggested. When Bergerac mentioned the twenty razor cuts, Liddell gave a grunt of surprise, which he tried to turn into a cough.

'Listen, Sergeant,' said Mrs Costain quickly. 'Just as a matter of interest, do you have anything to connect me

137

with all this, other than the word of a vindictive ex-employee who's no longer in a position to back up his story?'

Bergerac shook his head. 'His girlfriend arrived just in time to see him die, but I doubt if he told her anything. Anyway, the doctors say that it's fifty-fifty whether she'll say anything coherent again.'

'What a pity.' Mrs Costain smiled. 'Still, it'll teach her to pick her boyfriends more carefully in future.'

The remark was like a spark in a powder barrel. Bergerac would have attacked Mrs Costain physically, if Goddard hadn't restrained him by force. Neither of the policemen noticed Liddell's hand sliding inside his jacket, or the savage glare from Mrs Costain which stopped the bodyguard from going further.

'That's how you get your kicks, is it?' Bergerac had lost all control. Despite the size of the garden, the neighbours must have been able to hear. 'What sort of an animal are you?'

'Jim,' Goddard hissed. 'Cut it out, will you?' Crozier's reaction, if he heard about this, didn't bear thinking about.

'I should listen to your friend, Sergeant.' Mrs Costain chuckled. 'If I reported this conversation to your superiors, you'd be lucky if they'd still let you hand out parking tickets.'

Bergerac relaxed in Goddard's grip. His instinct for self-preservation reasserted itself: he'd achieved nothing by coming here – and risked losing everything. Mrs Costain's flat London voice continued to probe his weak spots.

'Fortunately,' she congratulated herself, 'I have a compassionate nature. I understand your feelings of guilt, Sergeant. You must have known the dangers you were leading Leech into, when you encouraged him to become a paid informer.' She shook her head gravely. 'I'm just sorry you're not prepared to face up to your responsibilities. Please don't try to ease your conscience by flinging wild accusations at me.'

She was clever, Bergerac thought, trying to distance himself from what was happening by analysing it. She knew that a relationship between a copper and a snout was a lot more than greed on one side and need on the other. It was a complicated, *personal* affair. Bergerac hadn't liked Leech – but he recognized that he had some sort of obligation towards him. And Costain was playing like a virtuoso on the fact that Bergerac had failed in his one elementary duty towards Leech – the provision of protection.

'Come on, Barry. Let's go.' Bergerac looked back at Mrs Costain. She stretched her body with a total lack of self-consciousness, like a cat waking up after sleeping off a good meal.

'Don't think this is the end of it, Mrs Costain. Believe me, I'm only just getting started.'

Neither Mrs Costain nor Liddell spoke as Bergerac and Goddard left the pool. The policemen walked through the house. The front door slammed behind them. A car engine came to life, revving high. Mrs Costain sat up. She looked venomously at her bodyguard.

'That was clever, Liddell, wasn't it? There they are, without enough evidence to hang their hats on, and you start reaching for an unlicensed revolver. Not just clever, Liddell – brilliant.'

'Sorry,' the big man mumbled. 'I – I wasn't thinking.'

'No,' his employer agreed thoughtfully, 'you're not with us at all, are you? What's the matter?'

Liddell said nothing. Mrs Costain stared into his pasty face for a moment. Apparently she found the answer there.

'You agree with that big brave sergeant, don't you?'

Her eyes narrowed. 'You think we should have finished him off quickly and cleanly.'

Liddell shifted in his chair. 'I don't know whether we had to – well – '

'You're all the same, aren't you?' Mrs Costain cut in. 'Big husks of bone and muscle – full of custard inside. Have you any idea what that little creep has cost me?'

The bodyguard could recognize the question was rhetorical. He rubbed a thick finger against the dark, shiny fabric of his trousers. His mouth was slightly open.

'I wish it had taken him ten times as long to die.' Mrs Costain's voice had changed. It was softer – and almost singsong. She might have been talking herself to sleep. 'I wish it had taken him a month.'

Chapter 14

For the next twenty-four hours, Bergerac worried his guilt over Leech's death like a loose tooth.

Even Crozier noticed – and the Chief Inspector was not the most sensitive of men. He came through to the general office late the following afternoon, just as Bergerac's shift was due to end.

'I've read your report,' he said abruptly. 'It's absurd to blame yourself.'

'It's true though – isn't it?' Bergerac looked sharply at Crozier. 'If it wasn't for me, Sam Leech would still be alive.'

'For God's sake, Jim.' Sympathy made Crozier sound irritable. 'You didn't even lean on Leech – just offered him a bit of spending money. He was free, white and twenty-one: he could have said no.'

'If you could have heard that Costain woman, Barney – '

'Now listen.' Crozier paced restlessly to and fro in front of Bergerac's desk. 'None of this is any good to anyone. If you've got Sam Leech on your conscience, the best thing you can do is start thinking about how we can nail the woman who did him in. Okay?'

'Okay.'

Crozier gave him a nod and left the office. On his way out he bumped into Peggy, who was carrying an armful of newspapers.

'What's all this? Trying to supplement your salary with a paper round?'

Peggy pursed her lips. 'I thought you might be interested, sir.' She handed him the *Evening Post*, pointing to the picture on the front page. 'We haven't heard anything official yet, but I remember you and Sergeant Bergerac talking about her.'

Crozier looked at the slim, blonde woman in the photograph and burst out laughing. He glanced quickly at the story to the left of the picture.

'You'd better show these to Jim.' He slipped the paper back on the pile. 'It's exactly what he needs.'

Bergerac was staring listlessly into space. Peggy dumped the bundle of newspapers on his desk.

'Chief Inspector Crozier thought you might want to look at these.'

Bergerac picked up the paper on the top of the pile. His face lightened as he looked at the photograph. The caption said: *Is This the Gentle Jewel Thief?* He picked up the next newspaper. The photograph was the same, but this time the caption read: *Ice Maiden With Heart of Gold.*

'I must say, she's very photogenic,' Peggy said distastefully. 'The story was on the news at lunchtime. They said there would be a full report on the six o'clock news.'

Bergerac glanced at his watch. If he left the office now, he should be in time to catch the news at home. He thanked Peggy and grabbed his jacket. Peggy watched him go. *Men*, she thought. *They're all the same.*

Once he got outside, Bergerac soon realized that he had been over-optimistic. It took much longer to get out of St Helier than he had anticipated; he had forgotten that it was the island's equivalent of London's rush-hour. His lips twisted in a grin. There was one house nearer than Susan's where he could be sure of finding a television, if not a warm welcome.

He turned into the curving drive of Hungerford's estate and drove up to the whitewashed Georgian mansion. The immaculate lawns and the neatly-regimented palm trees reminded him that he had promised to tidy up Susan's

142

garden. He leant on the front-door bell until Hungerford answered it.

'Hello, Charlie. Do you mind if I watch your telly for a few minutes?' He didn't wait for an answer, but pushed past his ex-father-in-law and into the sitting-room. 'Thanks,' he said over his shoulder. 'I knew I could count on you.'

The big television set was already on: Hungerford had been watching a cricket match. Bergerac changed channels and sat down in the armchair which Hungerford had just left. His host followed him in, with a bemused expression on his face.

'Weren't watching that, were you, Charlie?' Bergerac asked. There were a few seconds to go before the news started.

Hungerford bristled. 'As a matter of fact, I was.'

'It's just for a minute – I need to catch the news.'

Charlie snorted. 'Don't tell me that the upwardly-mobile Miss Young doesn't run to a television set?'

'I was just on my way home from the office – '

'Huh! So her place is definitely *home* these days?'

Bergerac grinned at Hungerford. The old man hadn't wanted an impoverished copper as a son-in-law; on the other hand, he took it as a personal insult that Bergerac, once divorced from Debbie, was still capable of taking an interest in other women.

'You were closer,' Bergerac explained.

Hungerford looked resigned. He crossed the room to the drinks cabinet. 'Glad to see you taking such an interest in world events again.'

Bergerac looked up. There was no mistaking the barb in Charlie's voice.

Hungerford continued: 'Someone on the committee was saying you'd been badly shaken up by what happened to this Leech fellow. Said you were blaming yourself for it.'

'Yeah, it did knock me sideways for a bit, but – '
Bergerac leant forward and turned up the volume on the television. 'Hang on – this is what I want to see.'

The news had already begun. The newsreader, staring fixedly at her audience of millions, was in mid-sentence.

'. . . unusual, to say the least. It began at one o'clock this morning with a phone call to the local ambulance service.'

The newsreader vanished, and a squat man in a dark-blue uniform appeared on the screen. He was looking with great embarrassment at the microphone in front of him. 'We got this call,' he said, 'from a lady with – you know – a rather plummy voice. Apparently her auntie had just had a heart attack. She described the symptoms, and I told her if she didn't give the old lady the kiss of life, she'd be dead before we got there. She seemed a bit reluctant, but she said she would. Well, when we got there, we found the old lady on the sofa and this really nice-looking blonde woman working on her. We took over. As soon as we told her that her auntie was going to be okay, the blonde went all funny – said she'd have to go upstairs and lie down for a bit.'

'Well?' prompted the disembodied voice of the interviewer.

The ambulance driver shrugged. 'That was it. We never laid eyes on her again.'

The newsreader reappeared on the screen: 'The victim, Mrs Harmer Harris, who has made a complete recovery in hospital, told the police that she has never had a niece; the "nice-looking blonde woman" was in fact a burglar whom she had surprised in the act of opening her safe. It was this shock which brought on the heart attack in the first place. Mrs Harmer Harris and the ambulance driver were both able to describe the woman. Police are anxious to talk to – '

144

The same photograph which the newspapers carried filled the screen.

' – Philippa Vale, whose name has been linked with several jewel robberies in recent years. Unofficially, she has become known as the Ice Maiden; ice, as all thriller addicts will know, is underworld slang for diamonds.'

The newsreader changed the subject and began to talk about the latest round of talks in Geneva. Bergerac switched off the set. Hungerford gestured with his glass towards the screen:

'Isn't Philippa Vale the one who lifted all those diamonds from poor old Maxwell Flagg?'

Bergerac nodded. Flagg was a notorious skinflint. There was a general feeling among the locals that Philippa Vale couldn't have chosen a more suitable victim.

'I thought you managed to get something on her.'

'So did we.' Bergerac got to his feet, jingling his car keys. 'We found the diamonds – she'd hidden them in the wreck of an old fishing-boat. We tipped off the Met about her. But by the time they caught up with her, the Powers-That-Be had decided that all the evidence against her was circumstantial – a clever lawyer would make mincemeat of us in court. So we decided that the best thing to do would be to wait and see if she ever came to pick up the stones.'

'And she hasn't?'

Bergerac had reached the doorway now. He turned back, his hand on the doorknob. 'Not yet – it's nearly twelve months now. But she's on the run at present. Maybe she needs every asset she can lay her hands on.'

Sergeant Murray whistled softly under his breath as he rotated the combination dial on the safe. There was a click as he hit the last digit. The heavy steel door swung outwards.

Murray added the file under his arm to the pile on the

bottom shelf of the safe. A faint sound from the doorway made him turn his head.

Constable Paris grinned awkwardly at him. 'Hello, Sarge.'

'What's the matter? Worried about your precious plates?' Murray patted the package on the top shelf of the safe.

Paris made a sound which was midway between a laugh and a sigh. 'I'm in enough hassle already,' he said. 'God help me if Costain got her hands on these plates.'

Murray closed the safe with a chuckle. 'She'd need an SAS squad to do that. It'd take the best peterman in the business a good twenty minutes to open that safe. And it's never left alone for twenty seconds.'

Paris nodded, but he still looked anxious. He shifted his weight from one leg to the other.

'Anyway,' Murray said reassuringly, 'there's a geezer from Holland coming to pick them up the day after tomorrow. I think we might manage to take care of them for forty-eight hours, don't you?'

'Yeah.' Paris caught the expression on the older man's face. 'Look, I know I'm being daft – '

'That's good. Recognizing your shortcomings is always the first step towards curing them.'

Paris laughed and left the room. In the corridor he met Bergerac, hurrying towards the Bureau's general office.

'Hello, Jim,' he said. 'I thought this was your day off.'

'It is.' Bergerac hurried over to his desk. 'I just wanted to check something.'

He dialled a number on his telephone and drummed his fingers while it rang. After nearly a minute the Docks Police answered. Bergerac asked for Goddard. There was another delay before he came to the phone.

'Barry? Any news?'

'Maybe. She may have come in on the Sealink ferry, but the uniformed man missed her.'

146

'What happened?'

Goddard sighed. 'There was a nun on the ferry, Jim. An hour after it docked, a lady turned up and said she'd found a nun's habit in the public toilet here. It was stuffed in the waste-bin. The only other person she noticed in the toilet was an old tramp who left when she arrived. She – the tramp, I mean – stank of meths, had a bad cough and hadn't had a bath for some time. Of course it may not be her.'

'We don't get many tramps here,' Bergerac said. 'Not that sort, anyway. Keep looking, Barry. I'd better keep an eye on the other end.'

At the other end of the phone, Barry chuckled. 'May the best man win.'

Until a few years ago, the lane had made a dog-leg at this point. Now the road ran straight, and the dog-leg had become a lay-by. Unkempt hedgerows sheltered it from the lane.

The big BMW was almost as wide as the lay-by. It squatted on the rutted surface. Smoked glass protected the privacy of those inside. As the minutes passed, the black, unreflecting surface of the car sucked in the sun's heat.

Mary Lou Costain turned in the passenger seat and looked out of the rear window. 'Where the hell is he?'

Liddell shrugged. 'Maybe he got cold feet.'

'He wouldn't be so stupid.' Mrs Costain's voice was cold.

At that moment a green Cortina, streaked with rust, pulled off the lane and came to a halt behind the BMW. Paris got out and, glancing nervously over his shoulder, walked towards the BMW. There was a *whirr* as the electric window rolled down.

'Get in,' Mrs Costain snapped.

'Look,' Paris began, 'it's too – '

147

'I said get in.' Mrs Costain unlocked the rear door on her side.

Paris scuttled into the car. He sat on the edge of the back seat, mopping his face with a grimy handkerchief.

'You blew it,' Mrs Costain snarled. Liddell turned in his seat and nodded his agreement.

'I don't know what else I could have done.' Paris swallowed convulsively.

Mrs Costain's face remained hard and blank. She was not a woman who tolerated failure. Paris felt the silence was smothering him. After a few seconds, it became unbearable. He tried to explain; the words came out in a gabble.

'I *had* to do it,' he said desperately. 'Otherwise they might just have kept a tail on him for days. You'd never have been able to make contact. I thought at least this way the plates would be where I might be able to get my hands on them. There was no way Van Rijn could have got them to you.'

'Can *you* get them to me?'

Paris swallowed again. 'They're in the safe at the Bureau. There's someone on duty there, right round the clock. And I haven't been able to find out the combination.'

Mary Lou Costain smacked the seat back with the palm of her hand. 'Then you'd better hurry up and find it, hadn't you?'

'There's a bloke coming from Holland to pick them up, the day after tomorrow.' Paris shifted back in the seat, in a vain attempt to put as much space as possible between himself and his employer. 'I could probably find out his flight times. Couldn't you just – '

'Paris!' Mrs Costain spat – literally as well as metaphorically: a drop of spittle landed on Paris's cheek; he hadn't the courage to wipe it off. She continued in a quieter but no less menacing voice: 'Apart from the fact that they'll

148

have him under police escort all the way to the airport, I can't wait forty-eight hours. I don't want to wait forty-eight minutes. You got the plates into that safe – now you can get them out. Is that understood? Or would you like Liddell to spell it out in words of one syllable?'

Liddell nodded ponderously at Paris. He lifted his right hand from the steering-wheel and clenched it into a fist, just to make sure that the policeman understood the message.

Mrs Costain jerked her head: the interview was over.

Paris fumbled with the door-catch. As he got out of the car, he said:

'I'll do what I can.'

'Yes, you do just that,' Mrs Costain said blandly. 'If you need any extra motivation, stroll down to the morgue and take a look at Sammy Leech.'

Chapter 15

The little cove was only a short drive from St Helier, but it might have been on another planet. The road ran round the cliffs; but the only way to reach the cove itself was on foot.

The bus grumbled up the road and drifted to a halt at the bus-stop. Only one passenger got out – an old lady who carried a grubby paper-bag. The driver started to ask her where she was going – it was a lonely spot, and the woman didn't look the type for long walks and communing with nature. But he gave up when the woman started coughing. Waves of foul breath, scented with methylated spirits, washed towards him.

The woman seemed in no hurry to go wherever she was going. She stood by the road, watching the bus until it was out of sight. Only then did she waddle over to the head of the path down to the cove. She paused there for a moment, checking that the road was empty.

When she reached the beach, she threw down the bag and began to pull off her clothes. First she removed the long shawl with ragged ends which had covered her head. Then she tugged off three filthy jerseys and a blue shirt with an unfashionably large collar. Finally she kicked off her shoes and unzipped the long, oil-stained skirt. The slender, blonde woman, dressed only in a white bra and pants, bundled her discarded clothes into a heap on the sand. There was a smile on her face as she ran down to the water.

The clear, warm water was a welcome relief after those foul clothes. She swam out towards the mouth of the bay, using a steady, tireless breaststroke. Every fifty yards or so, she would roll on her back and stare up at the line of cliffs which fringed the bay. Except for the gulls and one or two passing cars, she could see or hear nothing.

The sandbar lay across the mouth of the bay, just as she had remembered. The tide was ebbing now; the hulk was clearly visible beneath her. At the low-water mark, its salt-stained timbers would be exposed to the sun. It had been a working fishing-boat once; it had foundered in a winter storm a few years ago.

The woman dived smoothly down to the wreck. She grasped the gunwale with one hand and ran the other beneath the thwart in the centre of the boat. Where the thwart met the ribs, it was supported by a wooden knee.

Panic assailed her. Suppose it was no longer there? Anything could have happened to it in a year. Then her outstretched fingers touched something wedged between the knee, the thwart and the side of the boat.

Lack of air forced her to surface for a moment. The cove was still empty of human life. She dived again and tugged the sausage-shaped package out of the recess. It was reassuringly heavy. She tucked it into her bra between her breasts and swam back to the shore.

She crouched down on the sand, gratefully conscious of the sun's warmth on her back. It took her a couple of minutes to remove the outer oil-skin wrapping – she should have remembered to bring a knife. Inside was the chamois leather pouch. It was perfectly dry. She untied the thong which secured it and upended the pouch over the palm of her hand.

A dozen brightly coloured marbles rolled out. Most of them fell on to the sand. She stared incredulously at them. Suddenly a shadow slid across the sand and covered them.

'Miss Vale. Ever had that feeling you've been somewhere before?'

Philippa looked up. A man was standing over her.

151

Despite the fact that the sun was behind him, she recognized him at once. Sometimes – oddly enough – she had dreamed about him. She had only met him once, and that was nearly a year ago.

'Sergeant,' she said after a split second. 'What a lovely surprise. Jersey wouldn't be the same without seeing you.'

Bergerac helped her up. 'I knew you wouldn't want to leave without popping in to say hello. So I thought I'd save you the trouble.'

'How very thoughtful.' Philippa's smile gradually faded. She had a strange feeling that Bergerac wasn't enjoying this much more than she was.

'I never thought this moment would come, Miss Vale, but I think it's time I read you your rights.'

'What's the charge?' Philippa pulled herself together. 'Drunk in charge of a bag of marbles?'

Bergerac grinned. 'I think we can do better than that.' He glanced down at her ragged clothing and cleared his throat awkwardly. So he found her near-nakedness almost as disturbing as she did.

'Don't worry,' Philippa said brightly. She bent down and picked up the paper-bag. 'I never travel without a formal little number for being arrested in.'

The dress was simple and expensive; it had the further merit of not creasing easily. As Philippa pulled it over her head, Bergerac turned politely away. When she was ready, they walked up the path to the road. Philippa wondered miserably when she was likely to get her next swim. At the same time, she was trying to work out how this disaster could have happened.

'It was clever of you to work out where I'd left the stones, Sergeant. I suppose the case came back to your mind when you read about my little fun and games on the mainland?'

Bergerac nodded. He led the way over to the Triumph

152

and opened the passenger door for her. 'I told the port authorities to keep their eyes open for anyone who could conceivably have been you.'

'Ah . . .' Philippa got into the car with a mock sigh. 'And here was I thinking you'd been haunting the beach ever since I left – like Heathcliff dreaming of Cathy.'

Bergerac chuckled. He got into the car, but made no move to start the engine. Instead, he stared out over the sea. 'What were you going to do next?' he asked. 'Head back for the mainland?'

Philippa said nothing. Bergerac's smile broadened.

'You've got contacts on the island, haven't you? There's someone lined up to help you on the next stage of your journey.'

Philippa looked out to sea as well. 'It's a gorgeous view, isn't it?' In the same tone, she continued: 'Seriously, Sergeant, who would I know on Jersey? I was just going to treat myself to one last glass of champagne on British soil, and then be on my way. And that's your cue, I suppose.'

Bergerac's mouth twitched. 'Cue?'

Philippa cleared her throat and replied in a passable imitation of his own voice: 'Afraid it'll be a long time before you drink any more champagne, Miss Vale.'

Twenty-five minutes later, Diamante Lil eased the cork from the bottle of Moet and filled Philippa's glass.

Bergerac smiled at her. 'Thanks for opening the bar early, Lil.'

'My pleasure, Jim.' But Lil's attention was elsewhere – on Bergerac's guest. Her eyebrows wrinkled. 'We've met, haven't we?'

'Miss Vale is an acquaintance of mine in the jewelry business.'

Lil set down the bottle on their table. 'Haven't got any free samples you don't know what to do with?'

'I'm afraid not.' Philippa smiled back. 'I'm taking early retirement.'

Lil left them. Bergerac could tell she was still puzzled.

Philippa pointed at the label on the bottle. 'What's this? It's vintage champagne. Am I supposed to start sobbing on your shoulder after one glass and confess to everything I've ever done?'

'Something like that.'

Philippa's face became serious. 'You could get into a lot of trouble for doing this, couldn't you?' She raised her glass in a toast to him. 'I remember thinking you were pretty straight for a copper.'

Bergerac sipped his orange juice. His eyes met hers. 'And you're pretty classy for a thief, Miss Vale.'

'You mean Mrs Harmer Harris?' Philippa shrugged. 'You can't believe everything you read in the newspapers.'

'I suppose the truth is that you held her down and tried to throttle her until the ambulance men came and dragged you off.'

Philippa did her best to sneer. 'The truth is I went soft for five minutes – and we both know where that got me.'

Bergerac said softly: 'So of course you'll know better next time.'

Philippa could find no answer to that. Bergerac was smiling at her. For an instant she hated him for his perceptiveness. Policemen were meant to solve crimes, not to indulge in amateur psychology.

'I'm afraid you have to face it, Miss Vale – you've got style, whether you like it or not.'

'And that's what counts at the end of the day?' Suddenly Philippa found herself smiling back at him. She raised her glass. 'All right – to style.'

At that moment Charlie Hungerford bustled into the club. Bergerac turned away. He could hear Hungerford talking to Lil at the bar; he was reserving a table for this evening. Then Hungerford's voice dropped to an inaudible whisper. Bergerac cursed – almost certainly Charlie had recognized Philippa and was telling Lil all about her. He turned back to Philippa.

'Style,' he said. 'Yes, you've always had that. Your file makes that clear. I think I know it by heart now. I even did some digging on my own – I wanted to find out *why* you became the Ice Maiden. And I think I found out.'

He stared across the table at her. She found herself looking away. He continued in a quieter voice:

'Your father was an artist. The fashionable set took him up and then dropped him with a bang when the next craze came along. He started on heroin and couldn't stop. When the money ran out, there was only one way you could find to pay for his treatment. It was also a way of getting your own back on the rich idiots you blamed for what had happened to him.'

'Really, Sergeant,' said Philippa coolly, 'anyone who can weave theories like that out of a handful of facts ought to be working for a national newspaper.'

She finished her glass. Bergerac poured her another. Philippa gave him a sudden grin.

'All right,' she said. 'He was a good artist, you know. And he's still a nice man. I expect a big, strong, silent type like you wouldn't have thought much of him.'

Bergerac flicked the rim of his glass with his forefinger. 'Ask me why I'm not drinking champagne.'

'What? I thought you were on duty and policemen – ' She stopped and her eyes widened. 'Really? You mean . . . ?'

Bergerac nodded.

'Well, well. Who would have thought it.'

Hungerford, his curiosity at fever-point, was now making his way to their table. 'Afternoon, Jim.'

'Hello, Charlie.' Bergerac knew there was no point in

prevaricating. 'I don't think you know Philippa Vale, do you?'

The direct approach caught Hungerford by surprise, but he made a swift recovery. 'Only by reputation.' He smiled at Philippa; a pretty woman, in his view, remained a pretty woman, whatever she had done.

'I was just taking her down to the station to charge her,' Bergerac said smoothly. 'Only she – she was feeling a little faint.'

'Oh dear.' Hungerford turned to Philippa. 'Still, you seem to be making a remarkable recovery.'

'Two more glasses,' Philippa told him gravely, 'and I'll be as good as new.'

Hungerford's next words made it obvious that he thought Bergerac was wasting his time gallivanting when there was more serious work to do. He asked if there was any progress in the Costain case. Bergerac stonewalled him. Hungerford kept his temper with difficulty and returned to the bar.

Philippa watched him go. 'Who was that?'

'My ex-father-in-law. He also happens to be chairman of the Law-and-Order Committee. It's not an ideal combination.'

'What a lot I'm learning about you in such a short time,' Philippa said lightly. 'Tell me, who's the "Costain woman"? My local competition?'

Bergerac's face became bleak. 'Not exactly.'

Half an hour later Bergerac paid the bill and escorted her back to the car. They drove in silence through the outskirts of town towards police headquarters. Philippa rummaged in her paper-bag and produced a lipstick.

'You don't mind, do you? A girl always likes to look her best.'

'I doubt if there'll be any TV cameras waiting.'

Bergerac's eyes were on the road; the traffic was heavy.

Philippa put a dab of lipstick on her mouth. Keeping her eyes on Bergerac's profile, she tore a scrap of paper from the bag. On it, she wrote HELP in large red capitals. She wriggled in the seat, as if to make herself more comfortable. The manoeuvre ended with her leaning against the window; the scrap of paper was jammed between her shoulder and the glass.

It was a desperate plan, but it succeeded beyond her expectations. Bergerac pulled out to overtake a lorry. A minute later, the lorry roared past them and forced the Triumph off the road. Bergerac braked just in time.

He swore and leapt out of the car. Two men jumped down from the lorry's cab and grabbed him, one on each side. Before he could say anything, they hurled him back over the bonnet of his car.

Philippa, meanwhile, had got out of the car, allowing her dress to ride up as she did so. 'Please,' she said tremulously, fixing her large eyes on her two protectors. 'Don't let him hurt me.'

'Don't worry, love,' said the burlier of the two truckers. 'He won't lay a finger on you.'

Philippa turned and ran. She darted through the traffic to the other side of the road, and disappeared into a side street.

Bergerac made an instinctive move to follow her. The truckers tightened their grip. The larger one held a ham-like fist in front of his face.

'Right,' he said menacingly. 'Give me one good reason why I shouldn't smash your face in.'

'How about six months in the nick?' Bergerac's face was contorted with pain. 'I'm a copper, you dozy great lummox!'

It was just as well that Philippa took pains to keep herself fit.

She had less than a minute's start over Bergerac – and

he had the advantage of knowing St Helier like the back of his hand. After a quarter of a mile she found herself in a crowded shopping precinct. She slowed her pace to a fast walk; her dress might be suitable for being arrested in, but it was not designed for running inconspicuously.

Suddenly she stopped. At the far end of the precinct were two uniformed policemen; one of them was talking into his radio. It was more than possible that Bergerac had managed to put out an alert for her already. She was uncomfortably aware that it would be unwise to underrate his efficiency. She began to retrace her steps. After a few yards she stopped so abruptly that a fat middle-aged woman cannoned into her from behind.

Bergerac had appeared at the other end of the precinct.

Philippa ducked behind the fat woman, muttering an apology. There was only one route open to her – a side road which led off to the left. Bergerac, she could see, was now moving purposefully into the precinct.

She darted into the side road. It was a straight, narrow street, lined with shops. Before she had gone thirty yards, she realized her mistake. When Bergerac drew level with the entrance of the side street, he would inevitably glance down it.

And there was nowhere she could hide.

She looked desperately around her – and realized that the street offered dozens of hiding-places, inside rather than outside. Most of the shops were still open. She pushed open the door of one of the smaller ones. The sign over the window said ORIENTAL IMPORTS.

A bell jangled harshly over her head. The heavy glass door swung shut behind her. The shop was narrow but went back a surprisingly long way. It was cluttered with Far and Near Eastern artefacts, some of which had probably been made in Birmingham. Philippa tripped over the trailing hose of a hookah. It was dark in here. She picked her way between a pile of Turkish kilims and a dusty display of china. There was a curtained archway at the back of the shop.

The curtain was twitched aside. A tall, dark woman came into the shop.

'Can I help you?' she asked. The voice was harsh and unmistakably cockney.

'No thank you,' Philippa said. 'I'm just looking.'

The woman's eyes narrowed. She glanced down at the newspaper lying on the counter by the till and then back at Philippa.

'Upstairs,' she snapped.

Philippa frowned, playing the part of the innocent shopper. Her breathing sounded unnaturally loud to her. 'What did you say?'

'Through the curtain and straight up the stairs.' The woman held open the curtain. There was a sneer on her face. 'Unless you *want* them to catch you.'

For an instant, Philippa hesitated. She looked back at the window: the street offered no refuge. Then she hurried through the archway. The curtain swung back behind her.

Chapter 16

The shabby little room at the head of the stairs was furnished partly as an office and partly as a sitting-room.

Philippa sat on one of the hard chairs, her back straight. The woman had stayed downstairs. The minutes passed slowly. She was not alone – a fat slob who called himself Liddell was lounging in one of the easy chairs. His eyes never left her. Some men had bedroom eyes; Liddell's were hard-porn Soho. The intensity of his stare, the way he licked his lips and the slab-like hand which rested suggestively on his crotch made her increasingly uncomfortable. Perhaps it was a mistake to have come here – not that she had had much option. At least Liddell wasn't the talkative type.

She lifted her head as she heard footsteps on the stairs. The tall dark woman came into the room.

'The fuzz have gone,' she announced. 'Nowhere in sight.'

'Good.' Philippa rose to her feet, hoping her urgency wasn't obvious to her hosts. 'In that case, I think I'll – '

'No, don't rush off, Philippa.' The woman was still blocking the doorway. 'You don't mind me calling you Philippa, do you?' She nodded contemptuously towards Liddell. 'Don't tell me this lazy slob hasn't even offered you a drink?'

'I *did* offer.' Liddell's lard-coloured face hardened with anger. 'She wasn't interested.'

'Well, you'll have one now, won't you?' The woman went over to the drinks cabinet in the corner. 'There's no point in turning down a free drink.'

Philippa cleared her throat. 'I was always taught that

there's no such thing as a free drink. Especially when you don't know who's buying.'

'I'm Mary Lou Costain.' The woman looked sharply at Philippa. 'Does the name mean anything to you?'

She picked the words of her reply with care: 'I seem to remember hearing your name around town, a few years back.'

Mrs Costain handed Philippa a glass of neat whisky. She poured another for herself, but not for Liddell. Philippa took the smallest possible sip and tried to forget that there was already more than half a bottle of champagne in her stomach. In a brittle, social voice, she asked what her hostess was doing on Jersey.

'I retired here eighteen months ago.' Mrs Costain's eyes never left Philippa's. 'I run a nice, respectable business, of course. But more to the point: what are *you* doing on Jersey?' Before Philippa had time to answer, Mrs Costain turned to Liddell. 'The bottle's empty,' she said curtly. 'Go and get some more whisky.'

Liddell looked at his employer with undiluted hatred in his face. Philippa realized that his reaction was partly due to her presence: at the best of times, being ordered about by this woman must dent his macho sensibilities; the dent must be ten times worse when another woman, whom he was trying to impress in his own charming way, was a witness to it.

After a long, painful silence, the bodyguard got to his feet and stalked out of the room. Mrs Costain turned back to Philippa.

'Good little puppy, isn't he? But he needs his nose smacked from time to time. Now. You were going to tell me why you've come to Jersey.'

'I came to pick something up.'

'Something valuable?'

Philippa shrugged. 'I had a certain sentimental attachment to it.'

161

'Did you get it?'

'As it happens, no.'

'So.' Mrs Costain pursed her thin lips. 'You need three things: a place to hide from the law, a route off the island, and as much spending money as possible to help you on your way. Rather lucky you came through my door, wasn't it? I can offer you all three. Twenty grand in cash. What do you say?'

Philippa laughed. 'I'd say Christmas is getting earlier every year.' She put down her glass. 'Naturally, I'm assuming you're offering all this out of the kindness of your heart.'

'You're the one who specializes in sentimental gestures.' Mrs Costain's expression showed clearly what she thought of them. 'What I've got in mind wouldn't be difficult – it's not outside your usual run of work.'

'Diamonds?'

Mrs Costain shook her head. 'A safe. I want you to bring me its contents.'

'I've done safes in my time,' Philippa admitted. 'But I'm not exactly the best in the business.'

The older woman ignored her guest's modest disclaimer. 'There's only one problem,' she went on. 'Getting *to* the safe may be harder than getting *into* it.'

Mrs Costain explained. Philippa began to laugh.

As soon as Liddell returned with the whisky, Mrs Costain sent him out on another errand. He walked round to the theatrical costumiers with his mind seething with strong emotions. It would have been difficult to ascertain whether lust or loathing was the stronger. Liddell didn't even try: he was not a man who went in for self-examination.

The parcel, wrapped in brown paper, was waiting for him. He walked back through the hot streets, brooding on his injuries. He was sure Mrs Costain had got worse lately. The London Syndicate who had put up the money for the plates were leaning on her because she hadn't made the delivery to them on schedule. She was on edge: and that seemed to bring out the bitch's nasty streak – not that it was ever very far from the surface.

Worst of all, Costain had humiliated him in front of the blonde piece with the posh voice. He wanted that girl more than he could remember wanting anyone before. She needed to learn who was boss. He drifted off into a delightful fantasy in which he taught her the first lesson.

The fantasy dropped away from him when he reached the shop. Mrs Costain was behind the till. She told him to take the parcel up to the girl.

Upstairs, Philippa took the parcel but repelled his attempt to make conversation. He pretended to leave, but lingered outside on the landing. She didn't close the door behind him. Her back was turned to him. As he watched, she ripped open the parcel. When she saw what was inside, she laughed aloud.

Philippa unzipped her dress, revealing one slim brown shoulder. Liddell was entranced. Suddenly she whirled round and saw him standing there. She marched towards him. He found himself giving ground. Those cold eyes reminded him momentarily of Mrs Costain's.

'*Sweet* of you,' she said. 'But I've been able to do up my own buttons since I was a little girl.'

The door was slammed in his face. Behind him, there was a snigger. He swung round. Mrs Costain was standing at the head of the stairs.

'Eyes bigger than your tummy, Liddell?'

He grunted with anger and tried to push past her. But she gripped his arm. Her fingers were surprisingly strong. She lowered her voice, but the gloating tone remained:

'They don't call her the Ice Maiden for nothing, you know.'

The remark stung Liddell's pride. He said thickly: 'That – that's just a front.'

Mrs Costain sniggered again. 'Fancy your chances, do you?'

This time Liddell had the sense not to reply.

Mrs Costain became brisk: 'In that case you'll be pleased to know that I want you to drive our little guest to her appointment. Then wait and pick her up. Make sure she hands over the plates to you straight away.'

'All right.' Liddell's voice was grudging but he conceded that Costain was right: business was business. If the Syndicate didn't get the plates, his head would be on the block as well as Mrs Costain's.

'And then' – Mrs Costain's grip tightened on Liddell's arm – '*kill her*.'

Liddell's mouth opened, but no sound came out of it.

Mrs Costain smirked. 'Can't see any point in handing over twenty grand for no reason – can you? And there's another thing: she knows too much about my business activities.'

Liddell recoiled against the wall. 'You're truly sick,' he muttered. 'You do know that, don't you?'

'And then what?' Crozier asked.

Bergerac spread his hands wide. 'I've given a full description of what she's wearing to the airport, the docks, everybody. She can't get off the island.'

'Famous last words.' Crozier stabbed the Vale file with his biro. 'You know what that woman's like. This is just like the Flagg case all over again: she's making us look a bunch of clowns.' He waved aside Bergerac's attempt to interrupt. 'What makes it all look *really* terrific is you treating her to a bottle of champagne, just to wish her *bon voyage*. If the papers ever get hold of that – '

'How did you hear about that?' Bergerac burst in. This was going to be worse than he'd anticipated.

'I ran into Charlie Hungerford.' Crozier paused. 'Believe it or not, he wasn't trying to drop you in it: he didn't even know she'd got away. What the hell did you think you were playing at?'

'Does it matter? The only difference would have been that she'd have pulled the same stunt an hour earlier.'

'Maybe.' Crozier looked suspiciously at Bergerac. 'You're sure you didn't drink any of that champagne yourself?'

Bergerac counted slowly to five before replying. 'Is that all, Chief Inspector?'

'For the moment.' Crozier waited until Bergerac had his hand on the door-knob before adding: 'It all depends on whether we get her back, doesn't it? But if we don't . . .'

He allowed his voice to tail away. Bergerac could fill in the blanks: *certain disciplinary channels may have to be explored*, probably, or another of Crozier's bureaucratic formulas. He nodded curtly and left the office.

For once he got home before Susan. He put a Vivaldi tape on the music centre and made a quiche and a couple of salads for supper. Susan got back a little after eight. While they ate, they talked about what had happened to them during the day. Bergerac told an edited version of his meeting with Philippa Vale and its consequences.

Susan picked up the newspaper she had brought home with her. 'She's pretty, isn't she?' she said suspiciously.

'So-so.' Bergerac knew how penetrating women's intuition could be. He made a massive effort to be tactful: 'Of course she photographs better than she looks in real life.'

Susan shot him a shrewd glance and mercifully changed the subject. 'You seem remarkably cheerful for someone who's just blotted his copybook.'

'Oh, we'll get her,' Bergerac prophesied confidently.

'This is an island, remember. The odds are they'll have her in a cell before I get to work tomorrow.'

His confidence turned out to have been misplaced. Philippa Vale was still at large. Bergerac spent most of the morning out of the office, following up two reports of sightings. One was in St Ouen's Bay, the other near the airport. When he finally ran down the sources of the reports, both turned out to be artificial blondes who bore no resemblance whatsoever to Philippa Vale. Bergerac was not altogether surprised: a large proportion of police work consisted of following up false leads.

It was early afternoon when he got back to the Bureau; he had had no time for lunch. He bumped into Crozier as he went into the building.

The Chief Inspector looked sourly at him. 'You've had no more luck than anyone else, I suppose?'

Bergerac ignored him.

Crozier followed him up the corridor. 'It won't do, will it?'

'It's done though, isn't it?'

Bergerac imitated Crozier's intonation precisely. The Chief Inspector flushed slightly.

'That's all very well – ' Crozier broke off as he cannoned into an unusually trim WPC who was walking in the other direction. He muttered 'Sorry' to her retreating back and almost ran after Bergerac. 'You can make jokes about it,' he snapped, 'but a lot of people, including the press, are going to have a field day when word gets out about your little champagne session.'

Meanwhile the WPC rounded the corner and turned left into the security office. Sergeant Murray was behind his desk. With a skill born of long practice, he slipped a file cover over the paperback thriller he was reading. When he saw who it was, he relaxed.

'Sergeant Murray?' The WPC had a pleasant North

166

Country voice. Murray nodded. 'Oh *good*,' she continued. 'I thought I might have come to the wrong place. Chief Inspector Crozier wants to see you in his office right away.'

'Did he say why?'

'No. But he asked if you'd mind going down to records and collecting the Costain file on the way.'

'Typical.' Murray sighed theatrically, delighted to have the opportunity to display his professional knowledge to this remarkably attractive WPC. 'Peggy – his secretary – should do that sort of thing for him. It'll take me the best part of ten minutes.'

The WPC made a charming moue of sympathy. Murray gave her a paternal smile. He was about to leave the room when it occurred to him that he was leaving the safe unguarded.

The WPC seemed to read his mind. 'I'm supposed to look after things till you get back.'

'Good.' Murray's hand was on the door handle. 'Not seen you before, have I?'

'No, it's my first day.' The WPC looked helplessly round the office. 'Hope I don't make a mess of things.'

'Don't worry,' Murray said reassuringly. 'There's nothing to it. Anyway, you look like a bright little thing.'

The door closed behind him. WPC Philippa Vale, the newest recruit of the Jersey States Police, wasted no time. She pulled a bunch of skeleton keys from her uniform pocket and tried one after another until she found one which would lock the door.

Forty-five precious seconds evaporated. She had less than ten minutes to play with.

The safe was set in the wall behind Murray's desk. She ran her eyes over it, flexing her fingers. The make was familiar, and she had handled that type of combination-lock before. It would almost certainly be a six-figure combination. Given time, she was sure she could open it: her fingertips had had a lot of practice lately.

She hunched over the dial, straining to hear those tell-tale little clicks. As the minutes slipped by, her face became more and more strained. There were footsteps passing up and down the corridor. At one point, a set of footsteps seemed to stop outside the door of the security office. She forced herself to continue working, blocking out from her imagination what might happen if someone tried the door.

Urgency drove her to work faster. She was almost sure she had four of the digits now. She glanced at her watch: eight and a half minutes had passed.

There were two, scarcely perceptible clicks. Her fingers shook as they gripped the handle.

The safe was open.

Murray came up the stairs from records with the Costain file under his arm. He passed the door of the security office and was briefly tempted to pop in and see how the new recruit was managing. With her face scrubbed clean of make-up and her hair bundled under the uniform hat, she looked about sixteen.

He resisted the temptation. Crozier had a reputation as a martinet, and there was no point in provoking him unnecessarily. He could see the WPC afterwards.

A few yards along the corridor, he passed Paris. The Londoner was looking at his watch, as if he was waiting to meet someone. His face looked even more doleful than usual.

'What's up, Nick?' Murray said. 'Did your budgie die?' Laughing at his own joke, he carried on to Crozier's office. The door was closed. He could hear raised voices on the other side. Murray straightened his tunic and smoothed down his hair. He gave a token knock and went in.

Crozier looked up, his face tense. 'Yes?'

Murray felt puzzled. He held out the file.

Crozier frowned. 'Yes, *what*?'

'Sorry.' Murray swore silently. Senior officers could get so childish. 'Yes, Chief Inspector.'

Bergerac, sitting in the chair on the other side of the desk, stifled a laugh.

Crozier's frown turned into a scowl. 'Are you trying to be funny, Ted?'

'You wanted to see me, sir,' Murray said patiently. 'With the Costain file.'

'Who said I did?'

'She did, sir – the new WPC.'

Bergerac's head snapped round. 'What WPC?'

Murray took a step backwards. *Typical*, he thought: *you do what you're told to do, and then you get blamed for it*. Aloud, he said: 'I don't know. I'd never seen her before. She just said – '

Crozier and Bergerac exchanged startled glances. They pushed past Murray to the door, cutting off the sergeant in mid-sentence. They ran down the corridor towards the security office. Murray lumbered after them, still carrying the Costain file.

Bergerac was the first to reach the door. He tried the handle: it was locked.

'The key, Ted – *quick*,' Crozier snapped.

Murray fumbled in his pockets. The file he was carrying made him even clumsier than usual. As he searched, he tried to justify himself: 'Look, how could I know? She knew my name, she knew yours – '

'Just give me that key,' Crozier roared. He snatched it out of Murray's hand and tried to insert it in the lock. After a second he gave up. 'She's blocked the keyhole.'

Bergerac shouldered Crozier out of the way. 'All right – let me try.' He kicked hard, just below the lock of the door. The door held firm. He tried again: this time there was a crack and a split appeared in the door-frame. The third kick wrenched the lock out of the frame. The door flew open, crashing into the steel filing cabinet behind it.

The three men rushed into the room. There was no one there. The door of the safe sagged open, drawing their eyes like a magnet.

Crozier crossed to the window and looked down. 'She can't have flown out.' There was a thirty-foot drop down to the courtyard.

Bergerac was already moving towards the door. 'She didn't have to fly. She just walked out. She locked the door on the way out to keep us busy – the double-crossing cow.'

Crozier hurried after him into the corridor. Suddenly he stopped, as the implication of Bergerac's words hit him.

The double-crossing cow.

Chapter 17

The WPC with a package under her arm walked smartly down the steps from the Bureau, nodding to a couple of uniformed men who were going in. She crossed the courtyard and emerged on to the road. The black BMW was thirty yards away, parked on the opposite side. As soon as she appeared, its engine started.

The BMW was to her right. The WPC turned left. She paused beside a prosperous-looking, middle-aged man who was in the process of locking his dark-green Volvo.

She smiled up at him. 'Excuse me, sir. Is this your car?'

He nodded.

'Well, sir, a car answering this description has just been reported stolen.'

'What?' The man straightened up, with the keys in his hand. 'That's ridiculous.'

'I'm sure it is, sir.' The WPC's voice was soothing, almost maternal. 'I'm sure we can sort it out in five minutes. If you just let me have the keys I'll drive it round to the pound while you answer a few questions.'

The WPC removed the keys from his hand, opened the door and climbed behind the steering-wheel. As she started the engine, the Volvo's owner tried to protest. The WPC gave him an angèlic smile.

'Thank you *so* much for your cooperation.'

The Volvo shot off down the road. The BMW was trying to do a U-turn and failing because of the heavy traffic. Bergerac and Crozier came sprinting across the courtyard into the road. The middle-aged man immediately accosted them.

'I say! One of your policewomen has just driven off in my car. Had some nonsensical story about it being stolen.'

Bergerac watched the Volvo as it skidded out of sight round the corner. He turned back to its owner. His face was expressionless.

'Well, sir,' he said slowly, 'I'm afraid she was perfectly right.'

The next half-hour was a nightmare. Crozier organized an island-wide alert for Philippa Vale and the green Volvo. Bergerac, meanwhile, was detailed to take care of the Volvo's owner, who proved to be a wealthy Guernsey businessman. The man took a lot of soothing down. ('I shall make a formal complaint, you realize. I'm a personal friend of the chairman of your Law-and-Order Committee.')

It was Peggy who saved Bergerac from the seemingly-endless tirade of Mr Reginald Daubeny-Smith. She came in with a message from Crozier. The Chief Inspector wanted to see him at once.

'Thanks for the rescue, Peggy,' Bergerac said as they were walking down the corridor.

'I'm not sure it was a rescue,' she murmured. 'I think you're going out of the frying-pan into the fire.'

Crozier was on the phone when Bergerac reached his office. '. . . don't give me any excuses,' he was snarling into the receiver, 'I want it done *now*.'

He slammed down the phone and looked across the desk at Bergerac. 'Right,' he said softly. '*Double-crossing cow*. What's it mean?'

'All right,' said Bergerac wearily. 'It was a set-up.'

'Go on.'

'We fixed it up at *Lil's Place*. I let Philippa Vale escape, and she was going to run straight to the Costain woman.'

Crozier leant forward. 'And then what was going to happen?'

'I don't know.' Bergerac shrugged. 'We were going to take it from there. Maybe she could get something on Costain. I figured that Costain would think that a professional safe-cracker was a gift from heaven. She wouldn't be able to pass up the chance of getting her hands on those plates.'

'Ah.' Crozier's voice was silky. 'So you knew this was going to happen?'

Bergerac shook his head. 'I knew it *might* happen. But Vale was meant to get in touch with me first. The idea was that we could tail Vale from here and catch Costain in the act of receiving the plates.'

'Have you gone completely off your trolley? Why on earth should she do anything to make our job easier?'

'Because I told her the judge would take it into consideration. And because when I told her what Costain had done to Sam Leech, she didn't like it any more than I do.'

Crozier's eyes rolled towards the ceiling. He controlled himself with a visible effort. 'Look, Jim: Philippa Vale may have a winning way with old ladies, but she's a crook – first, last and in the middle. And crooks don't turn copper's nark unless it's the only course left open to them.'

'She went to Costain, didn't she?' Bergerac protested.

'Oh *sure*, she went to Costain. Why not? Then she comes here and double-crosses you – and Costain as well, by the look of it. She can't have her diamonds, but now she's got a highly desirable set of plates to boost her retirement fund.' Crozier's voice had been steadily rising; by this point he was shouting. 'Our only chance of catching her now is if she's laughing so much she gives herself a hernia.' Crozier glanced at the door to make sure it was closed. 'I thought you were sweet on her the last time she was here.'

'Oh, don't talk horse, Barney – '

'All right,' said Crozier grimly. 'Give me another reason for assuming you're not completely round the twist.'

For a moment Bergerac said nothing. There were reasons, all right, but not the sort they taught you about in police college. They made perfect sense to him, but he had a shrewd suspicion that Barney Crozier would consider them to be puerile rubbish. But he had to try to explain. Maybe Crozier could stop thinking like a policeman for a few minutes. Bergerac doubted it.

'Okay,' he said slowly. 'Philippa Vale blows her whole life away to stop an old woman dying of a heart attack. Mary Lou Costain tortures people to death, just for the fun of it. At the end of the day, I'd rather risk losing twenty Philippa Vales if there was a chance of nailing one Mary Lou Costain.'

Crozier made no reply. He was fiddling with a pencil. Suddenly it snapped in two. He looked up. 'Go home.'

'What do you mean? Am I off the case?'

'Jim.' Crozier arranged the pieces of pencil so they were precisely parallel on his blotter. 'Unless you can come up with a miracle in the next few hours, you're off the force.'

The telephone was ringing.

Bergerac was trying to work off his frustration and rage on Susan's overgrown garden. He had so far succeeded in cutting a small clump of nettles and one finger. His left arm, from shoulder to wrist, throbbed where the nettles had stung him in their death throes.

He threw the sickle at a bramble bush and ran into the living-room. He scooped up the receiver. When the pips stopped, he snarled his name into the phone.

There was a lady-like chuckle at the other end. 'Hard day at the office, dear?'

'That is not funny, Miss Vale. Nothing you do or say is funny.'

'What's the matter?'

Bergerac nearly put down the phone. Instead he said: 'We had a deal, remember?'

'Oh *that*.' Philippa still sounded amused. 'You don't think I'd be ringing you if I meant to double-cross you, do you? If you only knew the trouble I've had, getting hold of your number!'

That had puzzled Bergerac. The phone was listed in Susan's name. They had the number at the Bureau, of course, but it was standard practice not to pass on home phone numbers to members of the public.

'I rang your ex-father-in-law,' Philippa explained. 'I told him you'd managed to recover some jewelry of mine, and I wanted to thank you personally. I'm not sure he was altogether convinced.'

'Oh my God, Philippa – ' Bergerac could imagine with painful clarity what would happen if Hungerford mentioned the mystery caller to Crozier.

'And now, Sergeant, I'm going to tell your fortune. You're going on a journey over water. And you're going to meet a tall woman with blonde hair.'

Bergerac spluttered into the phone. He spluttered even more when Philippa told him precisely what she had in mind. But in the end he agreed to do what she wanted. After all, it could hardly make matters worse.

He had a quick wash, changed his shirt and drove down to the beach. There were plenty of people enjoying the afternoon sun, but he could see Philippa nowhere. He followed her instructions and hired a pedalo. The attendant looked at him curiously, but Bergerac tried not to notice.

The ungainly orange craft rocked violently as he climbed into it. He pedalled awkwardly out to sea, convinced that everyone was staring at him. He followed the line of the headland, keeping well away from the rocks. The water churned beneath him. The pedalo

175

provided very small results in return for a very large expenditure of effort.

He stopped pedalling, and the pedalo drifted to a halt. It rocked gently. Bergerac scanned the beach again. Where was she?

A sound behind him made him turn round. Another pedalo was coming round the headland. Philippa was pedalling vigorously. As she drew nearer, he saw that she had a broad grin on her face.

When the pedalos were about ten yards apart, she held up her hand. 'Isn't this fun! That's far enough, as they say in the cowboy films.'

Bergerac stopped pedalling. 'I suppose there is some point to this – other than making me look a complete Charlie?'

'Oh, every point. If you get any silly ideas about arresting me, you're likely to end up with nothing more than a nasty chill.' Philippa folded her arms. 'You do look annoyed.'

'I can't imagine why.'

'Neither can I. Everything went according to plan.'

'Except for one tiny detail,' Bergerac snapped. 'You were supposed to get in touch with me *before* you helped yourself to the plates.'

Philippa looked apologetic. 'Yes, I know. But I'm afraid when it came right down to it, I couldn't see myself as a copper's nark.'

'Pity you didn't develop those scruples before I let you make a run for it.' Bergerac was unable to keep the bitterness out of his voice.

'You don't understand. I promised to help you fix the Costain woman – right? Well, she *is* fixed. Her loathsome sidekick got drunk last night and I managed to prise a few details out of him. In a funny way, I think he was trying to impress me. The point is, Costain paid for those plates in advance. She's mortgaged every asset she's got to do it – including her house and business. She'll be lucky if they even let her keep her handbag.'

Bergerac shook his head. 'It's not good enough, Philippa. I can't see Sammy Leech's ghost sleeping easier at the thought of Costain spending a few months on the dole.'

'*And* she borrowed a quarter of a million from an organization in London – who are very anxious to have their investment back by the end of the week, at the latest. They're the sort of people who have their own special brand of Official Receiver. If you lean on her now, she'll probably confess everything in exchange for police protection.'

There was a moment's silence. A small private plane whined over their heads. The waves lapped against the hulls of the pedalos. Some children were having a race on the sands.

'I hope you're right,' Bergerac said. 'What about the plates?'

Philippa grinned. 'Some friends are looking after them for me.'

'I thought you didn't have any friends on Jersey.' Bergerac stopped. What was the point? He had never believed that particular story. 'You will return the plates, won't you?'

'Naturally,' said Philippa primly. The word meant *Of course not*.

'Naturally,' Bergerac repeated. 'I just hope you mean that.'

Philippa's eyes met his. For once they were completely serious. 'If I don't, you're in big trouble. Is that it?'

'What do you think?' He patted the side of the pedalo. 'I'll be lucky if I can get a job looking after these things.'

She hesitated. Suddenly she smiled and began to pedal furiously in the direction of the shore. 'Come on,' she called back to him. 'Last one to the beach is a wimp.'

Bergerac won the race by half a length. The attendant came to pull the pedalos out of the water. Bergerac was amused to see that the man looked at him with respect, rather than curiosity, now that he was with Philippa.

They walked a little way along the beach. When they were out of the earshot of other people, Philippa stopped. She scuffed her toe in the sand.

'I'm sorry – I got a bit carried away this afternoon.' The grin re-emerged. 'Every well-brought-up English girl wants her own police station to rob. And I did enjoy the uniform. I hadn't thought about where it would leave you.'

'I'll survive – as long as you *do* hand over the plates.'

'All right – don't go on about it. I said I would. I'm already beginning to hate myself, and it isn't even morning yet.'

Against his will, Bergerac laughed. Philippa's sense of humour was infectious. He just hoped the disease wouldn't prove fatal.

He tried to introduce a more business-like tone to the conversation:

'It's ironic: if you're right, all this has been a waste of time. We could have just sat on the plates, and Costain would have gone down anyway.'

'I wouldn't bank on it. She has contingency plans. If I were you, I wouldn't let those plates out of my sight until the man from Holland comes to collect them.'

Bergerac looked sharply at her. Philippa's warning might mean just what it said; but something made him irrationally certain that there was a sub-text beneath her words. After all, there were still puzzling features about the events of the last few days. For example, why hadn't Costain turned up to collect the plates, if they meant so much to her? He wished Philippa would tell him straight out what she meant. But perhaps that would be asking too much: she didn't want to be a copper's nark. After

Sammy Leech, Bergerac wasn't sure he wanted to be a nark's copper.

'Any more sisterly advice?' he asked, laying a slight stress on the *sisterly*.

She nodded. 'If I were you, I'd rely on my own judgement from now on. Ignore the Classically-recommended sources.'

'That supposed to mean something?'

'Think about it.' Philippa turned away to look out over the sea, effectively ending this stage of the conversation. 'It's nice here, isn't it? I wouldn't mind living on Jersey.' She looked at her watch. 'I really must be going. I'll ring you and tell you where you can pick up the plates.' She started to walk along the shore, confident that Bergerac wouldn't try to arrest her – not if he wanted to get the plates back.

'Philippa!' Bergerac said urgently. 'Come on, you don't want to spend the rest of your life on the run.'

She looked back. 'Sergeant, do you remember the first time we met? Last year? You told me then that nobody can have everything they want.'

Bergerac called after her: 'I'll wait for you to ring at the Bureau.'

'I thought you told me never to call you at work.'

She walked away, gracefully and quickly. Bergerac stood watching her, his hands in his pockets and a smile on his face. As the distance between them increased, the smile faded.

Chapter 18

'Oh look! There's the sea!'

The girlish enthusiasm in Mrs Pringle's voice was at least half a century younger than she was. She braked sharply, throwing Susan forward against her seat-belt, and pulled over to the side of the road. The baker's delivery van, which had been trying to overtake Mrs Pringle's Aston Martin for the last two miles, was forced to make an emergency stop behind them. The driver flashed his lights; he pulled out and overtook with his horn blaring.

'Really!' Mrs Pringle said severely. 'Young people have *no* sense of road courtesy.' Her face softened as she stared out over the crowded beach. 'How nice to see the sea again.' She made it sound as if she hadn't seen it for several decades.

Susan suppressed a sigh. It was difficult to get very far from the sea on an island which measured nine miles by five. She had spent the last three hours showing Mrs Pringle over a property which included its own private cove. Mrs Pringle had spent ten minutes in the house; the rest of the time she had devoted to exclaiming with delight over the inhabitants of the rock pools which dotted the cove. Susan had missed her lunch; and she was beginning to suspect that the client wasn't the type to bother with afternoon tea.

Mrs Pringle was alarmingly energetic; she was an appalling driver; and her conversation was monotonously concerned with the sea. But she had to be humoured: she was showing every sign of being willing to pay the grossly-inflated asking-price of an estate which had been languishing on the estate agent's books for the past eighteen months.

'I do like those little boats.' Mrs Pringle pointed at the brightly coloured pedalos which were bobbing on the water. 'Perhaps I should buy some. One could use them for cocktail parties,' she added vaguely. 'Oh, do look! Two of them are having a race.'

An orange pedalo and a green one were making for the shore, following the line of the headland. In one of them was a tall man wearing jeans; in the other was a slender blonde in a bikini. Susan felt a stab of envy. It looked a lot more fun than working.

'The man will win,' Mrs Pringle announced decisively.

Susan gasped. Jim was meant to be working today. But the man in the pedalo certainly wasn't. And, unless Jim had a double on the island, nor was Jim.

The orange pedalo ran aground, followed, an instant later, by the green one.

'Told you so,' said Mrs Pringle.

The blonde stood up, and Susan recognized her: so Jim was cavorting with Philippa Vale. *And* she looked a lot better in real life than she did in her photograph. Jim was laughing at something Philippa had said. As Susan watched, they started to stroll along the beach, walking very close together.

Susan's vision blurred with tears.

Mrs Pringle let out the clutch with a jerk and shouldered the Aston Martin into the stream of traffic.

Bergerac parked in the courtyard at headquarters and went up to the Bureau's general office. He sat at his desk and pretended to read through the reports which had piled up in his in-tray. Several people glanced curiously at him, but no one came over for a chat. Word had obviously got around – and Bergerac was being treated as a pariah until proved otherwise.

It was lucky that Crozier was at a meeting upstairs for the rest of the afternoon; if Bergerac hadn't known this, he wouldn't have come back to the Bureau. No one else would have the seniority or the nerve to send him back home. The Bureau was much closer to the centre of action than Susan's house was.

His eyes were on the typed pages in front of him; his mind was elsewhere. Philippa had given him a clue, he realized; and he was beginning to suspect that its solution was far more important than the arrest of a petty jewel thief.

Peggy came through on her way back from the canteen. She noticed Jim and, after a momentary hesitation, crossed the office to his desk. Bergerac grinned up at her. The secretary's exterior might be rather prudish, but he was starting to wonder whether there might not be a kind heart lurking beneath it.

'Hello, Jim. I thought – ' She bit her lip. 'I mean – '

Bergerac rescued her from her embarrassment. 'It's all right. I'm just waiting for a phone call.' It was the first time she had called him Jim. 'You couldn't do me a small favour, could you?'

'Well – I expect so.' She was clearly uncertain about where her loyalties lay.

The telephone at Bergerac's elbow began to ring.

'Find Nick Paris for me.' Bergerac picked up the phone. 'Tell him I'd like a quick word.'

Peggy nodded and left.

There were pips: so Philippa was using a public callbox again. When they stopped, her voice came over the line:

'Sergeant? I've got your precious plates.'

'I'm glad to hear it,' said Bergerac drily.

'I thought it might be a nice gesture if I left them at our old trysting place.'

'Wherever you like. Listen, Philippa – '

The phone went dead.

182

Bergerac looked up to see Paris looming over him.

'You want to see me, Jim?'

'Yeah.' Bergerac dropped the phone back on its cradle. 'I've just found a way of getting myself out of the mess I'm in. Since you're in the doghouse as well, I thought you might like to share my good luck.'

'Great – thanks a lot.' Paris's eyes slid sideways to the phone; he must have heard the end of that conversation.

'Philippa Vale just rang me,' Bergerac explained. 'She's leaving the plates out at the cove where I first found her. I thought if we move fast enough we might be able to grab her as well.'

Bergerac was already on his feet, the car keys in his hand.

'Okay, Jim.' Paris hesitated. 'I – I'll just have to tell Parker on the desk. I was meant to be taking over from him.'

'Be as quick as you can.'

Bergerac went down to the car and started the engine. Paris was longer than he should have been; Bergerac began to drum his fingers against the steering-wheel. The timing of this was going to be crucial.

At last Paris came running out of the building. He flung himself into the passenger-seat of the Triumph. The car was moving before he closed the door.

'We should still be in time, shouldn't we?' Paris was panting after his exertions. The sallow face was even paler than usual.

'I hope so.' Bergerac cut into the traffic, wishing he hadn't fallen foul of the rush-hour again. Still, it would be the same for everyone. He glanced at Paris: 'I really wouldn't like that lady to get the horse laugh on me again.'

Paris's eyes were on the road. 'She's a cunning little bitch, isn't she?'

'Cunning isn't the word for it.' Bergerac dropped a

gear and overtook a couple of cars. 'Sometimes I think she's a magician. I mean, think about it: she's only been on the island for twenty-four hours – yet she manages to get hold of a police uniform, find out exactly where we're keeping the plates, find out the name of the sergeant in charge of them – it's incredible.'

'Amazing,' Paris agreed.

'How do you think she does it?'

Paris shrugged. '*I* don't know.'

Bergerac grunted. 'Nor me.' He overtook another car. The traffic was beginning to thin out. 'And then,' he said thoughtfully, 'there was that funny remark she made to me.' Out of the corner of his eye, he could see that his passenger was staring at him now. 'Didn't I tell you? I saw her just over an hour ago. And she made this really weird remark. She said if she were me, she'd ignore the Classically-recommended sources of judgement. What do you think she meant by that?'

'God knows.' Paris's laugh was like a finger-nail grating on an enamel bath. 'You know what women are like, Jim – they'll say anything.'

'Maybe.' Bergerac let the car travel another hundred yards before continuing. 'But it set me thinking. Her father was an artist, so she must know all about paintings. I used to have this girlfriend who painted. I remember once her taking me round a gallery and showing me this big picture – these three women with next to nothing on; and a bloke was sitting by them, holding an apple – '

'I've never had much time for dirty pictures,' Paris said tightly.

'Ah, but you'd have been interested in this one, Nick. It was called "The Judgement of Paris".' Bergerac looked quickly at his passenger. 'And I remember Francine telling me that there was a famous phrase in some book: *Give me the judgement of Paris*. Now why do you reckon Philippa Vale doesn't think that's a terribly good idea?'

'I don't know what the hell you're talking about.'

'Did you get through all right? You were so long I thought maybe you'd got a wrong number.'

'Jim – '

Bergerac overrode him. 'Of course I could be wrong, Nick. But I reckon that five minutes after we reach that cove, Mary Lou Costain is going to roll up to get her hands on those plates. And if she does, there's only one person on earth who could have told her. And then I'll hand Chief Inspector Barney Crozier a nice little package: Costain and the plates – and a bent copper into the bargain. I reckon I'll be flavour of the month – don't you?'

Paris turned away abruptly, and stared out of his window. But Bergerac caught a glimpse of his face before he turned. Judging by Paris's expression, it wasn't despair that he was trying to hide.

'What are you grinning about?' Bergerac snapped.

Paris looked at him. It wasn't so much a grin, but something between a sneer and a smirk. Bergerac suddenly realized he had made a mistake. His plan had been based on an assumption which had just been proved fatally wrong.

Fatal – for Philippa?

He jammed his foot down on the accelerator. 'Costain wasn't at the shop as we both expected, was she? That's why you were so long – you had to make two calls. *She was at the house.*'

Costain's shop was right in the centre of St Helier. But her home was in a suburb which was little more than five minutes' drive from the cove.

Paris showed his yellow teeth. 'I just hope your girl-friend's gone by the time they reach the cove. Costain really hates her.'

'You'd better keep hoping that, Nick. Because whatever they do to her, that's exactly what I'm going to do to you.'

The smirk disappeared from Paris's face.

Where the cliff-path came out on the beach, there was a
flat rock like a natural picnic table. It was close to the
point where the marbles had spilled on to the sand.

Philippa laid the package on the rock, adjusting it so it
was as central as possible. She bent down and took a
single red rose from her handbag. She set the rose
diagonally across the package and stood back to appreci-
ate her handiwork.

These little artistic touches were so important, she
thought. They helped to keep an element of fun in one's
work. Jim Bergerac, she was sure, would understand
perfectly. She grinned to herself: that, in a way, was his
professional problem – he understood too well; and that
could be a handicap for a policeman.

The hair on the back of her neck prickled faintly.

Philippa's grin vanished. She turned slowly to her left.

They were standing, one on either side of the entrance
to the path. Liddell had a heavy Colt automatic in his
hand.

'Sweet,' said Mary Lou Costain, looking at the rose.
'That's really sweet.'

Unlike Costain, Liddell wasn't smiling. He thumbed
off the safety-catch on the automatic.

Costain glanced at him. '*Now* kill her.'

When the shot rang out below, Bergerac had just parked
on the cliff-top. He had snapped one cuff on Paris's left
wrist, passed the other through the steering-wheel, and
was just about to snap it shut on the right wrist.

His face was suddenly rigid with fear. There was a
click as the other handcuff locked itself. The action was
instinctive: for a moment, Paris had ceased to exist as far
as Bergerac was concerned.

Then Bergerac was out of the car, sprinting for the head of the path.

Liddell ran his fingers down the arm to the wrist and felt where there should have been a pulse. There wasn't one.

'She'll never be any deader,' he said with all the certainty of long experience.

He got to his feet. The gun was still in his hand. He looked at Philippa, who was standing five yards away and looking as if she would have preferred it to be five miles. She was pale under her tan, and shaking uncontrollably.

Liddell gave her what he hoped was a winning smile. He gestured with the gun at the corpse of Mrs Costain. 'Don't waste time worrying about her, love. She'd have danced on your bones.'

'I just – I just wondered why – '

'These are why, darling.' Liddell scooped up the plates from the rock. He left the rose. 'Why waste your life taking orders from a crazy woman, when you can soak in the sun for the rest of your days?' His voice hardened. 'All right: up the path. Move.'

Philippa walked slowly up the path. The exercise seemed to steady her. The trembling stopped, though Liddell was walking behind her with the gun trained at the small of her back. When she spoke again, there was a touch of the old hauteur in her voice:

'I suppose there's some good reason why I'm being allowed to live?'

'Three reasons, love,' said Liddell hoarsely. 'First off, you've got an escape route lined up; second, if you haven't, you'll make a lovely hostage to make sure I get away; and third, if you play your cards right after I sell the plates – '

The bushes rustled on the cliff-face above their heads. There was a thud, followed by an agonized gasp. Philippa swung round.

187

The path behind her was empty.

She peered over the edge. Six feet below her, Liddell and Bergerac sprawled on the sand, both winded by the fall. Liddell levered himself to his feet. Bergerac hooked an arm round his ankle and tugged.

Liddell's reaction was immediate and accurate: his free foot lashed out, catching Bergerac on the side of his head. Liddell grabbed a jagged piece of rock and moved slowly towards his prey. He was smiling.

The Colt and the plates were still on the path where Liddell had dropped them. Philippa seized them both. Liddell raised the rock above Bergerac's head, poised to bring it down on his skull.

'*Freeze.*'

Liddell glanced up, saw the gun in Philippa's hand and became like a statue.

'Now.' Philippa waved the gun. 'Back away from him. Slowly.'

As Liddell moved back, Bergerac scrambled to his feet.

'Keep still,' Philippa said. '*Both* of you.'

Bergerac grinned up at her. 'And if I don't? You'll let me have it right between the eyes, will you?' He took a couple of steps towards her. Philippa's lips twitched, though the gun remained steady.

'Liddell,' she said. 'Catch!'

She threw down the package containing the plates. Liddell caught it automatically. He gawped up at her.

'Well, go on,' she told him impatiently. 'Or has the prospect of a life in the sunshine suddenly palled?'

At last Liddell got the message. 'Good girl,' he muttered. He was already running along the beach, at the far end of which was another path. He kicked up clumps of dry sand as he ran.

'Oh yes, *good* girl.' Bergerac made no attempt to

disguise his bitterness. 'Terrific girl. If that's your idea of – '

'Sergeant!' said Philippa tartly. 'Are you going to stand there all day throwing insults at me, or are you going to get after him?' Her face broke into a smile. 'The jewel thief – or the killer: you can't have us both.'

For a moment, it looked as if Bergerac would explode. Then he began to chase Liddell.

Philippa walked briskly up the path. Every few yards she glanced down to see the state of play. The distance between Bergerac and Liddell was closing perceptibly. By the time she was halfway up, Bergerac had brought the Londoner down with a flying tackle. From here, it looked as if they were two overgrown boys, romping in the waves. She reached the cliff-top and gave Paris a nod.

She followed the line of the cliff until she was directly above Bergerac and Liddell. Only the former's face was visible; Liddell's was being held under water. Finally, Bergerac allowed Liddell to get up. The big man collapsed on the sand like a stranded whale, coughing up water and sucking in air.

She cupped her hands over her mouth: 'You took your time about it.'

'Listen,' Bergerac called back. 'Give up. If I tell the court everything you've done, they're bound to go easy on you. You'll be out in a couple of years.'

'I've got a better idea, Sergeant. Have you any idea what those plates would fetch on the open market? Why don't you and I take a year off and do Europe together on the proceeds?'

'What?' Bergerac's confusion was almost comical.

'Not your style, is it, Sergeant? And prison uniform isn't mine. And that's what it boils down to at the end of the day: a question of style. We've got different answers.'

'Philippa – '

'Byee.'

The cliff-top was empty.

Bergerac was late.

His shift this week continued into the evening. He and
Susan had arranged to meet at *Lil's Place*. After what
had happened this afternoon, Susan had seriously considered not coming. Then it occurred to her that there
was no reason why she should mope at home, just because
Jim had proved to be a lying toad.

No – tonight she was going to have fun. And part of
the fun would be telling Jim exactly what she thought of
him, preferably in front of a large audience.

She reached *Lil's Place* at nine-thirty. She was half an
hour late, but Jim wasn't there. Business was still relatively slow, so Lil joined her for a glass of champagne.

'You're looking a bit down in the mouth, love.'

'No I'm not,' Susan said pettishly.

Lil was too wise to pursue the subject. 'Jim was in here
yesterday,' she said chattily. 'With this blonde.' She shot
a quick look at Susan. 'Don't worry, dear, it wasn't like
that. I can always tell with Jim, you know. Anyway,
Charlie Hungerford told me afterwards who she was.
You'll never guess who it was – Philippa Vale, the Ice
Maiden.'

'I know.' Susan felt slightly – not much – better. 'Jim
told me.'

Hungerford himself bustled across to the bar. 'Ah, Lil
and – er – Miss Young.' He was obviously bursting with
news, and even Susan's presence could not deter him.
'I've just had a word with the Chief. You know Philippa
Vale's escape? Apparently it was all a set-up. Jim was
using her as bait to catch a couple of forgers and a
bent copper. Both from the mainland, of course. The
Committee may raise the question of a Citation. That's in

190

confidence, naturally. I've always said our police are first-class.'

Hungerford caught sight of Deborah and Jerome at a table near the dance-floor. He nodded to Lil and Susan and dashed off to spread the news.

Lil and Susan looked at one another: they started to laugh at the same time. Lil was the first to stop.

'I'll have to love you and leave you, I'm afraid. Must have a word with Jean-Luc.'

A few seconds later, Bergerac slid into the chair where Lil had been. He looked appreciatively at Susan.

'Have I ever told you,' he asked gently, 'how much I like your style?'

He reached inside his jacket and produced a single, rather battered red rose. He laid it beside Susan's glass.